The Alchemist and the Angel

Joanne Owen

illustration by Jeremy Holmes of Mutt Ink

Orion
Children's Books

First published in Great Britain in 2010
by Orion Children's Books
This edition published 2011
by Orion Children's Books
a division of the Orion Publishing Group Ltd
Orion House
5 Upper Saint Martin's Lane
London WC2H 9EA
An Hachette UK Company

1 3 5 7 9 10 8 6 4 2

A catalogue record for this book is available from the British Library
Printed and bound in the UK by CPI Mackays, Chatham

ISBN 978 1 4440 0194 5

www.orionbooks.co.uk

The Alchemist and the Angel

Also by Joanne Owen

Puppet Master

Acknowledgments

To those closely involved in creating this book,
especially my editor Fiona Kennedy,
illustrator Jeremy Holmes and designer Dave Crook.

To Orion Children's Books, especially Jane Hughes,
Kate Christer, Nina Douglas and Alex Nicholas.
To my agent, Catherine Clarke.
To friends and colleagues, especially Susannah Nuckey.
To my parents, John and Joan, and my grandparents.
To James, Jesse and Lily; to Katie, Dan, Jack, Mollie and Tillie;
to Paul and Jayne.

To the city of Prague and her stories.

'Birthplace, bonny, abroad'
Lloyd James, 'Untold'

To Lloyd James.

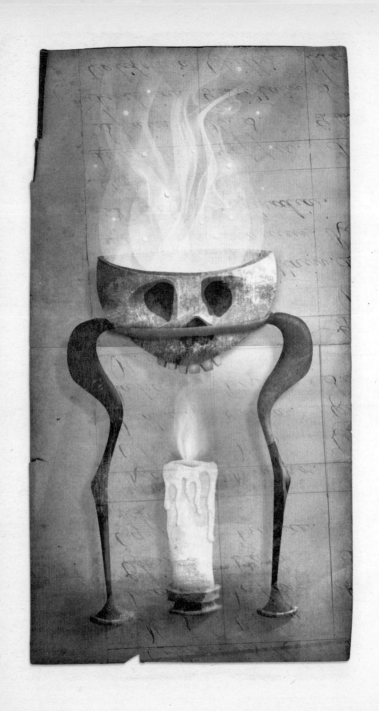

Contents

Prologue
The Heart of the World

Prague Castle,
Bohemia, 1583

mperor Rudolf II – Ruler of the World, Aficionado of
Alchemy, Collector of Curiosities – shifted in his
throne. The din of his retinue of astrologers and
astronomers, physicians and philosophers was driving him
mad. He could bear it no longer. Rudolf raised his hands to
his head, opened his mouth and released an almighty roar. It
echoed through the castle's maze of halls and corridors. It
infiltrated its innermost chambers. It could even be heard by
the prisoners held in Daliborka Tower.

The hall bristled with tension. Rudolf's eyes bulged red
with rage. His attendants fell silent. None dared look at him.
Tycho Brahe, the silver-nosed astronomer, examined his
watch. Oswald Croll, the physician, scratched the mole on his
chin. Michael Sendiv, the Polish chemist, stared at his shoes.
After what felt like an eternity, the roar diminished to a growl
and the Emperor heaved himself from his throne. He needed
to be alone.

Rudolf went outside to the cold calm of the castle

courtyards which formed a city within a city. A castle and a city whose towers and spires touched the stars, whose cellars and dungeons dug deep into the clay-rich soil.

The stars and the soil. The heavens and the earth. Rudolf had pondered the mysteries of the world and the universe since he was a boy. To him, the strange celestial events that had occurred throughout his life were no coincidence. But what did it mean that, in the year he turned six, there was a solar eclipse, two lunar eclipses, the passage of a comet and a mysterious conjunction of Jupiter and Mars? What did it mean that the death of his father and his coronation as King of Hungary coincided with the coming of a burning blue supernova?

Rudolf crunched through snow across Powder Bridge, over Stag Moat and towards the Royal Gardens. Dressed, as always, in the sombre black of the Spanish Court, his bulbous nose, plump lips and jutting jaw were typical of his lineage. His body was bloated by excessive banqueting, his eyes watery and loose-lidded. He stood not tall and confident like the world ruler he was, but with shoulders burdened by history. He'd never just been himself. Even as a child he was always known as the heir of Maximilian II, Emperor-in-waiting. First Hungary, then Bohemia, then ruler of an entire empire by the age of twenty-five, constantly preyed upon by the threat of invasion from without and revolt from within.

What if he hadn't been one of the Hapsburgs, destined to rule the world, at risk of succumbing to the sickness that had afflicted his family for generations? It had claimed the life of his grandmother, a woman now remembered as Joanna the Mad. He'd already seen signs of it in his eldest son, and he felt it in himself too. The itch of insanity that had led him to retreat into a world inhabited not by humans, but by oddities; his Cabinet of Curiosities. A series of chambers in Prague

Castle exhibiting his collection, the world's greatest natural and manmade marvels, everything from ancient relics to ostrich egg goblets and automated music machines.

Along with astronomy and alchemy, collecting was what made Rudolf happy. He mistrusted people. He could hear them now. Whispering voices. Murmuring in the walls. Rustling through leaves. He heard them everywhere he went. Everywhere, that is, except within the confines of his private chambers. Here the voices fell silent. He felt comfortable surrounded by his curiosities, for objects can't answer back. Objects can't betray.

Rudolf's craze for collecting included a zoo, in Lion's Court, just the other side of Powder Bridge. Among the menagerie of bears, wolves, wildcats and birds of paradise was the lion the Sultan of Turkey had presented to him. A symbol of sovereignty, the sun, and alchemy, this majestic beast was Rudolf's most cherished animal. Some years previously his chief astrologer had declared that since Rudolf and the beast shared the same horoscope they would share the same fate. And from that day forth the Emperor's lion ate only the finest meat, drank only the purest water and its enclosure was permanently heated.

An hour walking through the bitterly cold night froze his rage. Up here, high on one of Prague's seven hills, Rudolf had the world at his feet. He turned, looked back at the spindly gothic spire of St Vitus's Cathedral, where his father's body lay. He had many connections with this city. He knew it as a place of miraculous transformations. A place where chemists work to covert dirt into gold. A place where, locked away in their towers and caverns, alchemists seek to conquer death by developing an elixir of life. A place where practitioners of Natural Magick strive to decipher ancient symbols, harness the forces of nature and make the inanimate animate. A place, where, in short, the fantastical might be made real.

Rudolf stopped at the Singing Fountain, so named because of the musical ringing that sounded when its jets of water struck the bronze basin. He looked up and saw that the sky was clear, that the moon glowed silver above his observatory on the first floor of the palace. For once the signs seemed good.

Yes, he thought, *I will return the seat of Imperial power to Prague. I will make her the heart of the Empire, as she is ruler of my heart.*

But nothing is as it seems.

Rudolf knew the brilliant white snow shrouding the bridges and palaces of the Lesser Quarter hid deception and disease. He was aware that many of those who came to impress him with their displays of magic were charlatans. He knew something must be done to halt the spread of the plague in Prague's Ghetto district. And he knew that he would never escape the burdens of his birthright.

THE FIRST CHAMBER

Naturalia

Chapter One
In the House of the Seven Stars

Vienna, Austria
6th January, 1583

Several hundred miles away from Prague, in a tall thin house in the centre of Vienna, someone else had come to a decision. Doctor Gustav Grausam had decided to make his nephew his apprentice.

"Jan's been crippled by grief for too long," Gustav announced to his wife, Greta, after dinner. "He needs something to occupy his mind. It's time he learned the arts of alchemy and anatomy."

"Is he old enough?" she asked. "Is he *capable*? After all, you've never allowed me to . . ."

"Without a doubt. He's more than ready," Gustav replied, stroking his well-kept moustache. "And I need an assistant. Fresh blood to invigorate my work.

"I may be healthy," he continued, "but it can't be denied that I'm over halfway through my life. If I'm to realise the potential of my investigations I must have help. Together we could transform the scientific world."

"Stir yourself," called Gustav as he swept into his nephew's room next morning.

Jan turned to the wall, drew the bedclothes over his head. "It's still dark," he grumbled. "What time is it?"

"Time to start work," said Gustav, setting down a candle on the bedside table. "Scientists don't wait for the sun to come up. We rise before it, we work to understand how and why it behaves as it does. Besides, it will be light soon, so get up. I've decided to make you my apprentice."

Jan sat bolt upright.

"Hurry. I'll meet you in the cellar."

Jan didn't need to be told again. He jumped out of bed, pulled on his shirt and trousers, went to the dressing table. He caught sight of himself in the mirror. It was true what they said; he did have his mother's eyes. *Violet as juniper berries*. It was as if she were watching him now. He could hardly believe so much time had passed since she and his father had died. Nine months already. He missed them so much. His aunt and uncle were good to him but Jan often felt lonely. Uncle Gustav was always locked away in his cellar and Aunt Greta hardly left her rooms at the top of the house so he spent his days reading or exploring the city.

But perhaps things are changing, he thought, splashing his face with cold water.

While Jan had hoped he might learn more about his uncle's work, he hadn't dared imagine he'd become his *apprentice*. Minutes later, he was standing outside the laboratory.

"Come in, come in." Gustav waved him over the threshold. "Welcome to my Cellar of Science!"

Jan turned around slowly, trying to take it all in. First he noticed the black and white chequered floor, spread out like a gigantic chess board. Next he noticed the rows of dead birds hanging from the rafters, some preserved with their feathers resplendent, others stripped back to their skeletons. He looked to his right and saw a series of meticulously detailed charts of leaves, roots and flowers and anatomical drawings, among them a diagram of the human skull and musculatory system.

The remaining wall space was filled from floor to ceiling with shelves and drawers. A mass of stuffed mammals lined the top. Most were familiar to Jan – long-eared hares, foxes, squirrels, badgers, a bear cub – but there were also more unusual creatures; a blue-faced monkey, the head of a black-and-white striped beast that resembled a horse.

The shelf below displayed jars of preserved embryos. It was hard to tell from their undeveloped state but Jan thought they might be mice. Then came the *reptilia*, all manner of lizards and snakes organised according to size and species. The lower shelves were labelled with words whose meaning Jan could only guess at, like *conchiliata*, which exhibited various types of shell, and *lapides*, a collection of stones, rocks and gems. There were countless cabinets containing botanical samples – dried leaves, flowers, seeds and nuts. There were drawers of teeth, bones, horns and fur, and glass caskets bearing bizarre insects that had been varnished to protect their colours from fading. There was a corner devoted to *mariana*, things of the sea, like pieces of coral and hollowed out crustaceans, sea stars and turtles, and a cabinet filled with eggs, some so large and

exotic-looking that Jan supposed they must have been laid by rare birds from far-flung lands. His jaw dropped.

"Well?" asked Gustav. "What do you think?"

"I don't know what to say," Jan replied, shaking his head. "All these strange creatures. I know this is a wolf's head, and this a boar tusk and this an ibex horn," he said, pointing to the animal parts mounted above Gustav's head, "but I hardly recognise some of these. There must be more specimens here than in the city museum."

"Perhaps," said Gustav. "It represents a lifetime's work, but unlike the Imperial Library here in Vienna, or the royal Cabinets of Wonders of Ambras Palace, this isn't a museum for the dead. My interest is in the living. See for yourself," he said, pointing to a doorway in a far corner of the room. "Go through. But mind where you tread, no sudden movements and be sure to close the door behind you."

Jan did as his uncle asked and found himself in an enclosed garden. It should have felt cold – the pale winter sun was barely visible through the frost-covered glass roof – but it was as warm as a summer's day, as if the plants and flowers housed here were releasing heat through their lush leaves and uncommonly bright petals. A cluster of fruit flies circled his head, their bodies glistening like droplets of fresh blood. And as Jan waved them away, he thought of the long summers he'd spent in his father's orchard.

He hadn't really known Gustav then, but he'd always loved hearing tales of his uncle's life in the city. He was the only one of his family to leave their remote village for good, the only one who'd made a name for himself in the wider world and Jan had always quietly hoped to do the same one day.

It seemed a talent for medicine and science ran in the family. Jan's mother had been the village healer, entrusted with delivering babies and administering herbal medicine.

How cruel it was she'd lost her life through her work. She'd been poisoned by the plague while nursing a patient in the advanced stages of the disease. It seemed to Jan that it had come like an ogre. Grotesque and greedy, it had stomped into their cottage and infected his parents with its filth. They were dead and buried within days. The villagers had thought it a miracle that Jan was spared. And sometimes, on those days when his loss was too much to bear, when all he saw was the grassy path to his old home fading behind him and a stony track stretching before him, when all he felt was an ache in his heart, Jan almost wished the ogre had taken him too.

He loosened his ruffled collar and moved deeper into the garden. Dozens of dazzlingly plumaged birds darted through the tangle of leaves and flowers. A host of butterflies – some striped, others spotted, some that seemed to sparkle – alighted on his chest and shoulders until he'd all but vanished beneath their fluttering wings.

Jan jumped as a screech like the cry of a newborn infant rang through the garden. He felt a rustling at his feet and, all at once, an azure-bodied bird emerged from the undergrowth. It unfurled its train to reveal a shimmering fan of feathers. Its markings reminded Jan of lidless blue eyes, set in iridescent bronze and green rings. Jan had seen paintings of peacocks. He'd heard they were proud creatures, revered in ancient legends and kept by kings, but he'd never imagined he'd encounter one in real life, let alone in his uncle's house.

The Queen of the Gods and Her Hundred-Eyed Bird

Many years ago in Ancient Greece there lived a goddess named Hera. She was the queen of the gods and the heavens and of women and marriage.

When people thought of Hera they thought also of peacocks and cows and pomegranates, for these were her sacred symbols. Her wagon was drawn by a host of peacocks. Cows symbolised her role as mother, and the pomegranates represented a woman's love for her husband.

Hera's life was one of danger and drama, especially in matters concerning her family. For example, when she rejected one of her sons for being ugly, he made her a golden throne which, when she sat on it, held her prisoner with its invisible fetters. Here she remained until she promised to make beautiful Aphrodite his wife.

And Zeus, Hera's husband, the lord of the heavens and king of the gods, also brought great tempests to her family. He was a hot-tempered man, given to infidelity and so Hera employed a hundred-eyed giant to spy on him.

One day, the giant discovered Zeus with another woman. To escape Hera's wrath, Zeus transformed the woman into a cow. But Hera saw through his trick and asked for the cow as a gift. Since this animal was sacred to her Zeus couldn't refuse, and Hera kept the woman-turned-cow captive in a cave and ordered her giant to guard it day and night so Zeus had no opportunity to return the beast to its original womanly form.

Determined not to be outwitted, Zeus sent Hermes, messenger of the gods and lord of thieves and trickery, to recover the cow. Knowing it would be impossible to escape detection from the giant's eyes, Hermes played a mesmerising tune on his flute. One by one, the giant's eyes closed. As soon as the hundredth eye had closed, Hermes took an axe and chopped off the giant's head.

When Hera found her giant, all bloody and beheaded outside the cave, she removed each of his eyes and placed them on the tail of her beloved peacock so, wherever she went, she was protected by the hundred-eyed gaze of her favourite bird. And from that day on all peacocks have been blessed with these unique markings.

"I see you've found my gift for Greta. A beauty, isn't she?"

Jan stooped to examine the bird. Standing still as a statue, the creature fixed its shiny black eyes on him. Jan moved away, alarmed by the intensity of its stare. "Where did it come from? And how big will it grow?"

"No bigger than it is. It's the first of its kind, a new miniature subspecies I've created."

"You created it?" asked Jan. "How?"

"I knew you'd have an aptitude for this," Gustav said, smiling. "Curiosity breeds discovery. It began about seven years ago when a scholar I'd allowed to use my library thanked me with a clutch of eggs laid by an Indian Blue peahen. The eggs weren't much to look at, but I knew this belied the beauty of the beasts they contained. I took care of them until they hatched and grew into handsome birds, which in turn laid more eggs. I found myself enchanted by them, and wondered if it might be possible to make them even more magnificent, in the way certain species of dogs have been bred to sit at the feet of kings, or warm the beds of princes. I fed them nothing but the finest seeds and succulent grubs, and kept them in cosy pens. After tending several generations, I realised I'd created a new kind of peafowl, a diminutive subspecies in which both the male and female display these majestic markings. Usually only male peafowl – peacocks – bear this extravagant plumage but this is female, a peahen."

"But why did you want to make them smaller?" asked Jan.

"Sometimes scientists do things simply because they can, to see what might happen. Accidents can yield great discoveries," Gustav explained. "I didn't know what the outcome would be but, when it happened, I realised this bird was relevant to the rest of my work, which is all about growth and life and transformation."

Fig 7: PeaHen

"I see," said Jan, still not sure he really did. "But what exactly does this bird have to do with that?"

"The scholar believed that since they're of the air, birds are mediators between the earth and the heavens." Gustav raised his arms. "He claimed they facilitate alchemical transformations. We'll give this one to your aunt this evening. Perhaps it will cheer her."

"But what's everything else for? The butterflies, the plants, the birds. Why do you need them?"

"It will all become clear," Gustav promised, ushering Jan into the building and securing the door to the garden. "Follow me." He led Jan back through the laboratory to his library.

"So many books," Jan gasped. "I can't wait to read them all."

He knew he was lucky his mother had taught him to read; few people in his village had been able to. Books were costly; precious objects to be treasured, so he'd always looked forward to the parcels that had come from Vienna every birthday since he'd turned eight. He still had them – the bestiary illustrated with creatures from legend, encyclopaedias of astrology and ancient history, collections of myths from around the world – each volume carefully chosen by Gustav and always inscribed with the same dedication, *"For my nephew, Jan, that he might go forth into the world furnished with knowledge, aglow with the wonder of words."*

Jan hadn't forgotten that delicious moment between unwrapping the package and discovering what was inside, or the smell of the ink and paper that prickled his nostrils as he turned the first page. Then he'd savour it slowly, relishing every sentence, every illustration, every piece of wisdom. His mother used to joke that as long as he had a book for nourishment, Jan would never go hungry. He scanned the shelves, reached out and ran a finger across their spines, all the while thinking he would never be starved here.

"Have you read all these?" he asked.

"Of course, several times over, and many more besides, and you will too," replied Gustav, as though all that reading could be done in the blink of an eye.

Jan watched his uncle stride through the library, pulling books from shelves and adding them to the already towering piles stacked around the desk. Down here, in his laboratory, dressed in his billowing black robes, Gustav was master of the kingdom he'd created. Here he was transformed from Uncle Gustav into Doctor Grausam, renowned Anatomist, Natural Scientist and Creator of Zoological Curiosities.

"Lesson one," Gustav announced, sitting down at his desk. "Arthropods, in particular the anatomy of insects and Lepidoptera."

"Lepi ... Lepidoptera," Jan repeated, nervous he'd never learn all these new words. "What does that mean?"

"Butterflies and moths. Don't worry, in a few weeks you'll be well on your way to fluency in the language of science."

Some hours later, Gustav placed an arm across Jan's shoulders. "That's enough of that for one day," he said, closing the book they'd been studying.

"What next?" asked Jan, trying hard to stifle a yawn.

"Something you'll find more interesting, I hope."

Jan's cheeks burned radish-red. "I am interested, really. It's just we started so early and ..."

"Lesson two," Gustav interrupted. "The Conversion of Poisons."

He led Jan to a case of caterpillars. Jan watched them squirm, mesmerised by the rippling thin black-and-yellow stripes along their bodies.

"These may be small, but they can be deadly. They're from the New World. Every stage of their metamorphosis is dependent on a poisonous plant called milkweed. Their eggs hatch on milkweed, they feed on milkweed, as pupae they attach themselves to milkweed and eventually emerge as Milkweed Monarch butterflies."

"I've been working to transform their poison into something that could be used as medicine. This possibility was first discovered by Paracelsus, an alchemist I had the good fortune to study with. According to him, 'All things are poison and nothing is without poison. Only the dose determines whether something is poisonous or not.'" Gustav raised an eyebrow. "What do you think he meant by that?" he asked.

Jan thought for a moment, determined not to disappoint his uncle. His left eyelid twitched, as it always did when he was concentrating hard. "Does it mean that anything could be poisonous? It just depends how much you have."

"Exactly. In small doses, even lethal substances can be harmless. And the reverse is also true; too much of something as pure as water could kill you."

Gustav handed Jan a pair of gloves. "For protection. These butterflies are still toxic. Use the tongs to remove the specimen from the top compartment of that glass cabinet. Mind you don't damage it. That's it. You've a steady hand. Lay it on the dish and bring it here."

Jan looked at its markings; the brilliant orange wings, veined with black lines and tipped with white spots. "I'd no idea these could be dangerous. Back home, in summertime, the meadows are full of butterflies that look like these."

"Jan," Gustav said gently, "I know your aunt and I are no substitute for your parents, and nor can we ever be, but this is your home now. Don't forget that."

"I won't," said Jan quietly.

Gustav looked into the magnifying apparatus on his workbench and adjusted the settings. "And never forget that some of nature's most glorious-looking creatures and plants are also the most dangerous," he continued. "Don't be deceived by beauty. Now, place the butterfly beneath the lens and tell me what you see."

Wondering why he was being asked such a simple question, Jan pressed his eye to the rim of the viewing cylinder. "It's a dead butterfly."

"Dead. Yes, it's quite dead," Gustav agreed. He took a bottle from a drawer beneath the bench and dispensed a droplet of the fluid it contained onto the butterfly. "Keep watching and tell me if you notice any change."

Jan stared hard. "No. Nothing."

"Concentrate. Do you not see the hint of a flutter in the wings? A twitch of life?"

"Wait a minute ... Yes! You're right, it is moving. Look!" Jan stepped aside.

"Indeed it is," Gustav affirmed. "Or rather it was. It's fallen still again. The serum must need some modification. Only minor, I'm sure."

"Do you mean that tiny drop of liquid brought the butterfly back to life?" asked Jan. "How? What's it made from?"

"It's a concoction of processed plant and animal matter," Gustav explained. "It's what alchemists call Dancing Water, the Elixir of Life."

Jan couldn't believe his uncle's matter-of-factness. This was incredible, but from the way he spoke you'd never know Gustav had created a potion that could revive the dead! "But Uncle ..."

Gustav pressed a finger to his lips. "But nothing. Have patience. Do you think I learned everything in a single day?"

He put the stopper back in the bottle, returned it to its drawer then pressed something into Jan's hand. "This is for you. A key to our Cellar of Science."

Chapter Two
Her Beauty and his Beast

While Gustav had established his kingdom in the depths of the house, among the earth and roots, Greta Grausam's domain was in the eaves, some five storeys above the ground, closer to the clouds and stars. She'd become attuned to the rhythms of the sky-dwellers that rested the other side of her walls. By day cooing doves soothed her as she read or embroidered, and at night the flutter of bats' wings lulled her to sleep.

As dusk descended, Greta sat alone in her bedchamber before a mirror flanked by two flickering candles. She loved to be surrounded by opulence. Her rooms were furnished with silks, intricate tapestries and ornaments that sparkled. And each was suffused with the sweet musky scent of the rosewater she used to keep her skin soft.

Greta laid down her ivory hairbrush, raised a hand to her throat. She was paler than the choker of pearls displayed there. Gustav had given her the necklace on their wedding day, for her name meant 'pearl'.

She smoothed her arched eyebrows. She re-powdered her forehead and chin. She daubed her lips and cheeks crimson. Finally she glazed her face with egg white, fixing the powder and rouge, completing the magical transformation of skin and bone into a smooth shell-like mask.

Formula for ceruse, also known as Spirits of Saturn, to achieve a white complexion

Heat lead and ground marble in a furnace for three days, and mix the resulting ashes with green figs and distilled vinegar.

Formula for fucus facepaint to enjoy radiantly red cheeks and lips

Mix cochineal insects with the white of hard-boiled eggs, the milk of green figs, plume alum asbestos and sap from the acacia tree.

Greta stared into her grey eyes. They darted keenly – birdlike – from forehead to chin, from ear to ear, as she scrutinised her reflection. She knew most women would be more than satisfied with everything she had; a respected husband, a large house in the heart of Vienna, all the dresses and jewels she could wish for. But it made no difference. She couldn't shake the feeling that life was passing her by, that nothing she did really mattered. And more so now than ever, for while Jan had been made Gustav's apprentice, she remained outside his world, a world from which she'd long felt excluded, and she feared this would never change.

A knock came at the door. "Are you ready for supper, Mistress?" asked the serving girl.

"Thank you, Alzbeth. I'll be along shortly."

The dining room was laden with the aroma of roasted meats

and wood smoke. The table had been laid with a feast of roast venison, wild boar and baskets of bread made from the finest flour. At its centre, a silver platter bearing a suckling pig stuffed with a pigeon, and a jug filled with wine.

Jan stood at the hearth and poked the fire. The logs hissed, shot sparks of burning wood up the chimney. He went to the window, opened and closed the heavy drapes, then poked the fire again. He was restless to return to the laboratory.

"Will you show me how you make the serum tomorrow?" he asked. "And can we try to bring something else back to life? I'm not sure I really believe what happened to the butterfly. I mean, how was it possible? Unless it wasn't dead in the first place ..."

"I can assure you it was," said Gustav. "You saw for yourself, didn't you? If you're to become a real man of science you must learn to expect the unexpected."

"I will," promised Jan. "I'm sorry."

"No need for apologies. As I said this morning, it's good to question things, but you must have faith too."

The door opened slowly, sweeping a chill through the room. It was Greta. Silent as snow, and solemnly, she went to her seat.

"How are you this evening?" asked Gustav. "I trust you enjoyed your day. I was right. Jan has the makings of a fine scientist."

"I'm sure he does," Greta replied.

"It was unbelievable, Aunt Greta. I never thought such things were possible! I learned that not all poison is actually always poisonous, and that some ordinary substances can be harmful. Like this water," he said.

Greta watched them closely. Jan's whole demeanour was different this evening. He was animated, bursting with excitement at the new knowledge he'd learned. And she saw how proud Gustav was that his nephew had understood all he'd been taught. Her fears were confirmed.

"Aunt Greta? Uncle can create miniature versions of animals, and bring dead creatures back to life."

"Bringing the dead back to life?" said Greta dismissively, pushing her pewter plate aside. She'd always had a small appetite. "What kind of nonsense is that? Shame on you for making things up, Jan. I thought you knew better."

"Jan's right," said Gustav. "It's all true."

"What do you mean?" Greta said, frowning.

"I've developed a potion that reanimates lifeless matter. It works very well on reviving decomposing plants and today we tried it on a dead butterfly. It still needs some refining but, once perfected, it has revolutionary potential."

"Isn't this what alchemists seek?" asked Greta, her eyes widening. "The elixir of life?" She leaned towards Gustav. "Why have you kept it from me?"

"Because the serum hasn't yet been perfected," Gustav replied. "The butterfly only came back to life for a brief moment. I still have much work to do."

Exasperated, Greta stood and went to him. "If this is true, then your star is truly destined to ascend. This could bestow more power and esteem than owning all the world's wealth."

"I'll present it to the university when I'm ready," Gustav replied.

"We should think beyond that." Greta paused to catch her breath, tilted her head to one side as she pondered the options. "We must go to Prague, City of Alchemy and Gold."

Jan felt a shiver run through him.

"The Emperor has just announced he's moving the centre of the Empire from Vienna to that very place," Greta continued. "We should go. You could present your elixir to him! Haven't I always said you should have more ambition?"

"I'm not a jester. I don't perform tricks." Gustav was suddenly dismissive.

Jan fidgeted in his seat as he looked from Gustav to Greta.

"Greta, I insist everything you've heard this evening remains a secret until I'm ready to publish my findings," Gustav told her.

Eyes flashing, Greta turned to leave.

"Wait!" called Jan. "What about the gift?"

"Of course," said Gustav. "Don't go yet. I didn't mean to sound harsh but what good would it do to present a half-finished idea to the world? And besides, all kinds of unscrupulous men would love to get their hands on it."

He reached beneath the table and unveiled the gilded cage. "This is for you."

"For me?" asked Greta. "Such a beautiful creature."

"Uncle made it. It's a new kind of peahen."

"You made a new kind of *real, live* bird?"

"Indeed," said Gustav, "and you won't find another like it. This is the first of its kind. As Jan said, I've created a new subspecies."

"But how?" asked Greta.

"All you need know is that she's a unique creature, as distinctive and elegant as her mistress."

"Thank you. I'll treasure her," said Greta. "At last I have some part of your work."

She picked up the cage and went to the door. "I look forward to discovering more," she added, her satin shoes scarcely making a sound as she slipped across the wooden floor.

Alone again in her chamber, Greta placed the birdcage on her dressing table. She'd never imagined Gustav had been performing such incredible feats in this very house. Perhaps her life here wasn't yet completely doomed to dullness.

Greta sighed as she remembered their first months together, when she'd lived a charmed life. But how quickly Gustav's work had claimed him. However, this evening's talk of a death-defying potion had given her renewed hope.

Just then, her peahen gave a shrill cry. "Do you agree with me, my beauty?" Greta asked, opening its cage. "And did you see what happened down there today? Did you see the dead come back to life? Did you see how he did it?"

The bird fixed its gaze on her and, all of a sudden, Greta was overwhelmed with affection for it. It stepped onto the dressing table and nuzzled her hand with its crown of tufted feathers. "So tame," she whispered. "And loyal, I hope. You'll never desert me, will you?"

Two floors below, Jan was finding it difficult to sleep and lay wide awake, pondering everything Gustav had revealed. If the butterflies could be made harmless, could all poisons be eradicated? And what might it mean if the elixir of life was successful? Could all illnesses be treated?

During the course of this single day, all kinds of possibilities had opened up to him, and Jan wondered what tomorrow held in store. He reached for the key to the cellar he'd left on his bedside table, pressed it to his lips. He'd felt so happy when Gustav had said this was his home but now, alone again with his thoughts, he wasn't sure it would ever be right to feel completely at home here. His cottage and village would always be his real home, wouldn't they? To think anything else would feel like a betrayal of his parents. Jan wasn't sure what was right.

When he was younger, if he'd ever had trouble sleeping, his mother would tell him the tale of the day he'd been born. Jan closed his eyes and listened for her voice.

The First Coming of the Ogre and the Stars that Stopped Him

*O*ne morning a young woman named Mathilde awoke with a warm flutter in her heart, for she knew this was the day her first child would come into the world. Being the village wise woman, she was usually right about these things. For instance, Mathilde always could tell exactly what illness afflicted a person just by looking at them, and she always knew which herbs to administer to heal them. If a woman wanted to fall pregnant Mathilde knew to feed her hazelnuts, and if a person was suffering from melancholy thoughts she knew to feed them thistles. So, when she opened her eyes on that bright spring morning, there was no doubt in Mathilde's mind that her child would be born before the next rising of the sun.

After a breakfast of oatmeal and warm milk, Mathilde lined a cradle with a sack stuffed with fresh straw, ready to lay her baby on. Then she laid out a piece of rabbit fur, ready to swaddle her baby in. At dusk, certain the baby would be born in the next few hours, she asked her husband, a handsome young man named Johann, to prepare a warm bath for her. Then they waited together for the baby to arrive.

But by nightfall Mathilde knew something wasn't right. First she felt a coldness in her bones. Then came the limb-tingling, the brow-burning and a dull ache deep in her swollen belly. So she sent Johann to fetch Old Kunigund, the Herb Mistress who lived in a hut on the outskirts of the neighbouring village, some three miles away.

Johann couldn't have gone any faster but, by the time he'd stirred Old Kunigund from her bed, there was so much blood that the Herb Mistress advised him to go for the priest, fearing neither mother nor unborn child would survive the night. So Johann went into the sharp spring night, sick to his stomach with dread, when something very strange happened.

As soon as Johann set off down the path that led to the priest's house, dozens of crows fled the fir trees that loomed either side of him and swooped across the sky in a six-pointed formation. Shocked by this sudden movement and the menacing black shadows of the crows, the lambs in the meadow began to bleat, quietly at first but quickly rising to an excruciating crescendo. Johann raised his hands to protect his ears. And it was then he saw it.

A host of shooting stars burst through the silken fabric of the sky and exploded in a cascade of sparks, shedding blue and silver light across the horizon. Johann had never seen anything like it. But then a dreadful moan came from the cottage and Old Kunigund appeared in the doorway and beckoned him inside. Johann stumbled back expecting the worst, his heart aquiver. But, when he entered the cottage, he saw not the scene of death he'd expected but Mathilde the mother, all radiant and overflowing with joy, their newborn child asleep at her breast. And she named the boy Jan.

Not all Jan's dreams were happy ones and, hours later, he was jolted awake by a terrible noise. He rubbed his eyes, realising it was the sound of his own voice, screaming into the night – *No! Leave them!* He sat up in a cold sweat, his head throbbing with the horrors he'd seen, his hair – so blond it was almost white – stuck to his forehead. Still shaking, he lay back down and pulled the blankets close, trying his best to shake the feeling that he was being watched. Eventually, he fell asleep.

But the nightmare came again, and this time more cruel than before. Jan is in a clearing close to the family cottage. He can hear his mother singing as she kneads dough in the kitchen. He listens to his father chopping wood, each stroke as accurate and regular as clockwork. Then he becomes aware of the pounding of heavy boots on hard earth, and the dull clang of a bell sounding in time with every step. He sees the hunched form of a clothed beast lumbering towards the cottage. Jan wants to warn his parents, to run and save them, but he finds he can't move. He looks down and sees that his feet have become trapped in a tangle of spiky brambles. He sees the beast enter the cottage. His mother screams. His father rushes to her. Jan tries to cry out but no sound will come from his lips. He sees the beast emerge, then fade into the thick of the forest, dragging his parents behind it, the bell around its neck swaying erratically.

The sky is completely starless.

Chapter Three
The Root of Man

Jan lay in bed hoping Gustav would come for him soon. He waited and he waited until he could bear it no more. The draw of the cellar was too strong. Shortly before five, he got up and went to the laboratory. He crept quietly along the corridors, candle in hand, his shadow long and thin on the floor behind him.

Jan unlocked the cellar door and went straight to the workbench. He took the bottle of serum from the drawer and held it up to the candle. It was a murky reddy-brown colour and contained fine threads of what he supposed must be plant fibres. Then, very cautiously, taking care not to touch the glass with his bare skin, Jan sniffed it. To his surprise, it didn't have the strong chemical odour he'd expected. Instead it was earthy, like woodland after rain. He sniffed it again, this time inhaling more deeply, and detected a hint of spices, perhaps cinnamon and nutmeg, and wild roses.

"Careful with that," said Gustav as he entered the room, delighted to see Jan's keenness, but concerned that he appreciate the serum's value. "It's more precious than gold. Your dedication is commendable, your first day went well and your mother would be proud of you, but you have lots to learn today, so put the bottle back."

"Aren't you going to teach me more about the serum this morning?" asked Jan. "I want to understand how it works. Do you think it could be used to stop people dying of the plague?"

Gustav raised an eyebrow. "Once the causes of the disease have been identified, perhaps we could adapt it for that purpose."

Jan felt his heart skip. "*Really*? Do you mean it? What do you think causes it?"

"Well," Gustav replied, "doctors once thought it was transmitted by a certain type of flea, which is why a mass purging of cats was ordered when the disease first raged across the continent. But now some experts think rats could be responsible."

"But fewer cats would have meant there were more rats, so ..." Jan paused, "so killing cats would have made things even worse, wouldn't it?"

"Perhaps," said Gustav, "but we still don't know the exact role, if any, rodents might play. In fact, a respected physician recently suggested that birds and bad air might be to blame. That's why specialist plague doctors wear masks like beaks. They fill them with strong-smelling herbs and spices to protect them from the air and stench of sickness."

"Birds? What about the birds in your garden? Are they safe? And Greta's peahen?"

"They're all in excellent health; each a perfect example of its species."

Jan thought for a movement. "Do you think we'll understand all the causes some day, so it might be easily treated? Do you think that's possible?"

"As an alchemist all my work – and all yours too – is about sustaining and generating life," Gustav explained. "So yes, I do believe it's possible. But on with today's lesson. Yesterday you saw how life might be restored. Today you will see how life might be created."

"Creating life? But ..."

Gustav raised a finger to his lips – he didn't like to be interrupted while in full flow – and began to pace the chequered floor, arms tucked behind his back, head held high.

"You see, alchemists have three principle objectives. The first, the transmutation of common materials into gold or silver, is of little interest to me. Of course, the ability to transform something like copper into gold requires a degree of scientific expertise but has little immediate benefit to mankind. I shall leave this pursuit to my more materially minded colleagues."

"What's the second?" asked Jan; so far, everything his uncle had revealed had been the stuff of dreams.

"You were introduced to that yesterday. It's the search for a remedy to cure diseases and prolong human life, which is the purpose of my serum. And the third," he continued, reaching into a cabinet for a bundle of cloth, "the third is the creation of human life. Do you know what this is?" he asked, unwrapping the bundle.

"It looks like a withered old man," Jan shuddered, cautiously laying a finger on the object. "It feels fleshy too, like weathered skin. What is it?"

"It's the root of a type of plant. A mandrake, which means Dragon Man, but it's also known as Witches' Manikin, Brain Thief, Sorcerers' Root, Little Gallows Man and *Zauberwurzel*. It's long been used in magical rituals, largely due to its similarity to the human form, but its powers are beginning to be newly recognised by scientists today. Some say they feed from the blood of the hanged to turn into what Paracelsus termed a *homunculus*, an artificial man."

"What do you mean?" asked Jan, his left eyelid twitching.

"It's a plant that might be transformed into a man. Here, read this," said Gustav, handing Jan his notebook.

Methods of Homunculi Creation

The Sack Brew Method

(Note: This is a crude and primitive technique, not generally practiced by serious scientists).

Place the bones, dried blood, skin fragments and skin or fur of a selection of animals of your choosing into a cloth sack.

Surround the sack with fresh horse manure and bury it.

Leave it immersed in the earth for forty days, during which time an embryo should develop.

After forty days dig up the sack and release your creature, which will be a hybrid of the parts surrendered into it. For example, dogs' bones, boar skin and cat blood will form a dog-shaped creature with the bristles of a boar and the temperament of a cat. The combination of human bones and fish scales will produce a tiny human that can breathe only in water.

The Egg Method

Eggs possess an elemental power. Their outer shell is earth. Their white is water. The membrane that lines the shell is air, and the yolk at the core is fire. The core of the egg preserves life and being, and therefore represents heaven and earth, while the white represents chaos.

Instructions:

Take an egg laid by a black hen and poke a small hole in the shell.

Release a pea-sized quantity of egg white and replace it with human blood.

Reseal the hole with wax.

Bury the egg in dung on the first day of the lunar cycle.

Once it's had time to form – in thirty or forty days – a miniature human will emerge from the egg.

Feed the creature lavender seeds and earthworms and it will obey and protect.

WARNING: failure to care for the creature and feed it this diet may result in it turning on its creator.

The Mandrake Method

Instructions:

Uproot a mandrake on a Monday, day of the moon and her magic.

Slice off its roots and bury it that same night in a graveyard.

Return here every day for at least a month and nourish it with cow's milk in which a bat has drowned.

After a month has passed the mandrake may be uprooted and dried in an oven containing verbena (also known as vervain, Herb of Enchantment, Juno's Tears and Simpler's Joy), a plant renowned for its cleansing and healing properties.

Precautions to be taken when harvesting a mandrake root

When mandrakes are pulled from the ground, they release an unearthly shriek that can cause deafness, lunacy or even death to humans. To safeguard against this:

Stuff the ears with the wool of a pregnant ewe.

Go to the burial place when the sun is obscured, either when the morning mist is thick or when the moon is high and full.

Dig a ditch around the root until its lower part is exposed.

Tie a dog to the root and walk at least twenty paces from the burial place.

Tempt the dog towards you with a pail of bloody offal so it uproots the mandrake in its haste to reach the meat.

Once freed from the earth by the dog, humans can touch the mandrake with no fear of danger.

Mandrake Miscellany

They thrive best in rich soil, in the shade.

They are frequently found where the blood of hanged men has fallen to the earth.

They can be used to help barren women fall pregnant.

When crushed, the roots and fleshy orange berries of the mandrake plant can be used in love-inciting potions. Some cultures refer to it as the 'plant of love'.

Jan read and re-read the notes, to be sure he'd taken everything in. Then it dawned on him. "Are we going to use the mandrake to make a little man?" he asked.

"Yes," said Gustav. "That's exactly what we'll do."

Jan stared at his uncle, giddy with excitement and fear, as if he was standing on the edge of a cliff. "Why?" he asked. "Because we can?"

"Well remembered," Gustav said, "but no. It's because I wonder if combining a mandrake man with my serum might create an invincible being. A being so intelligent and strong and resistant to illness it will live forever."

He gripped Jan's shoulders. "Do you see? If this works, future generations won't have to waste time and lose lives while battling with individual diseases like the plague. They'll be resistant to all infection. We could be on the verge of unlocking the key to eternal life."

"Today is Monday," said Jan. "Shall we do it today?" he asked, his voice lowered to a whisper.

"We shall. I know a place where mandrakes grow."

Jan knew he was about to plunge over the cliff into the terrifying wonders of the unknown, and he couldn't wait.

Chapter Four
In the Village of Nuts

The carriage was drawn from the cobbled courtyard by a pair of handsome white horses, their wide nostrils exhaling great gusts of air as they trotted down the Street of the Seven Stars. Jan hadn't expected to see anyone out and about this early, but they passed several traders trundling barrows piled high with sacks of flour and wool, while others drove chickens to the market squares. Before moving here, he hadn't thought it possible for people to live so closely packed together. It was nothing like his village, where there were wide open fields to run through, and meadows he'd loved to lie in while the sun beat down.

Jan pressed his nose to the carriage window as the royal palace came into view. "Look at all the carriages gathered at the Hofburg gates," he said, pulling on Gustav's sleeve. "What's going on?"

"It must be to do with the Emperor's move to Prague," Gustav replied. "I didn't think it would happen so soon, but I suppose he is known for his rashness. What Rudolf wants,

Rudolf gets. I wonder if he'll take all his treasures with him, for his Cabinet of Curiosities in Prague Castle."

"His what?" asked Jan.

"His Cabinet of Curiosities, his pride and joy," Gustav replied. "Imagine a decorated cabinet carved from the finest wood and fitted out with dozens of drawers and cupboards and cases. Then magnify the cabinet. Imagine it's the size of a castle wing and, instead of drawers and cases there's a series of chambers, each displaying different kinds of objects. In one there might be priceless relics from the ancient world – Rudolf claims to own two nails from Noah's Ark and the dagger that killed Caesar – in another precious stones and shells, or the skeletons of rare beasts."

"That sounds like your laboratory," said Jan. "What does the Emperor's chamber have that your cellar doesn't?"

"One or two things," Gustav said, smiling. "His is said to be the most remarkable Cabinet of Curiosities the world has ever seen. Kings and sultans from far and wide are desperate to be invited to view it. The world's most skilled artists, goldsmiths, engravers and stone cutters vie to create pieces for it. But," he continued, "what I have could be far more valuable than Rudolf's treasures, however extraordinary they might be."

"What do you mean?"

"My serum of course, and our homunculus too if everything goes to plan. While Rudolf's patronage of art and alchemy can't be denied, and it's reported he's considering taking further action to halt the spread of the plague in Prague, his cabinets may as well be tombs. He collects for the sake of collecting."

Jan sat up straight. "What does he know about the plague?"

"Never mind the Emperor," Gustav continued. "We have

our own business to worry about. Here's a test for you. Tell me all you've learned about the mandrake method of homunculi creation."

In the time it took the carriage to rattle along Graben Street, where vegetable and flower sellers were setting up stalls beneath the spectacle of St Peter's Church, Gustav was satisfied Jan knew exactly what they were going to do. Prickling with anticipation Jan settled back in his seat as they continued past St Stephen's Cathedral and turned onto the Alley of the Beautiful Lantern, a narrow winding lane with a tale of greed to tell.

The House of the Basilisk on the Alley of the Beautiful Lantern

One morning, many years ago, a Viennese baker named Moritz was feeling very pleased with himself, for he and his dog were about to move into new premises on the Alley of the Beautiful Lantern. The building gleamed white as the flour Moritz used to make his dough, a well filled with an endless flow of freshwater stood in his courtyard.

"There's not another bakery like it in all Vienna," he boasted to his apprentice boy. "Imagine how twisted with envy my fellow bakers will be!"

While he lay in bed that night, imagining dozens of rich new customers praising his delicious breads and pastries, Moritz heard strange noises coming from his courtyard. First came a plop and a splash. Then came the scratch-scratch-scratch of sharp claws on stone. Then came a succession of squawks and croaks. But, supposing his mind was playing tricks on him after the long, tiring day, Moritz ignored the noises and went to sleep dreaming of the fame and riches he would enjoy as Vienna's most exclusive baker.

Moritz woke at sunrise, drew a bucket of water from his well and merrily prepared his wares. Once everything had been baked and laid out, he ordered his apprentice boy to open the doors. But no sooner had the first customers arrived than an uncommonly filthy stench swirled inside, causing their eyes to water, their noses to burn and their stomachs to churn. Moritz offered his customers a drink of the water he'd drawn from his well that morning, but this only made them worse, for somehow the freshwater had become as foul and filthy as a stagnant marsh and everyone who drank it fell sick. As soon as they were able, the customers fled the bakery, vowing never to return, leaving the baker beside himself with shame and anger.

"Someone must be plotting my ruination!" he snarled.

Just then, Moritz heard the wild howls of his dog coming from the courtyard. He and his apprentice boy rushed outside to see what the commotion was. When they reached the courtyard, where the stench was even more potent, Moritz saw his dog fall from the outer edge of the well and drop dead on the ground.

"Have they poisoned my dog too?" Moritz cried. "I wonder if these events have anything to do with the strange sounds I heard last night?"

"What sounds?" asked the apprentice boy.

"Well, first there was a plop and a splash. Then a scratch-scratch-scratch of sharp claws on stone and then a succession of squawks and croaks. I supposed my mind was playing tricks on me after my long and tiring day."

The apprentice boy turned whiter than the flour Moritz used to make his bread.

"What is it?" Moritz demanded. "Are you involved in this plot to ruin me?"

"I've heard about such creatures," the boy replied. "It must be a basilisk, a foul-smelling water-dwelling beast that's half-cockerel, half-toad. It has poisonous skin and a glance that kills and comes to curse the houses of the selfish and greedy."

"Then I'm doomed," cried Moritz. "If the gaze of this beast has the power to kill, how will I remove it from the well and save my business from ruin?"

"Don't worry," replied the apprentice boy. "If you promise to be generous and kind and give up your greedy ways, I know a way to get rid of it."

"I swear I'll never be greedy again," said Moritz the Baker.

So the apprentice boy ran down the Alley of the Beautiful Lantern and returned with a mirror. He climbed down the well, holding the mirror before him and when the basilisk saw its own reflection it turned to stone and never bothered the baker again. That is, until the day he forgot his promise to always be generous and kind...

Gustav and Jan crossed the Danube Canal as the first signs of the new day were becoming visible. Wisps of hazy reds and violets seeped through the night sky, spreading like ink through silk.

"We're almost there," said Gustav.

Jan sat up straight and saw a sign bearing the coat of arms for the village of Nussdorf at the roadside.

"The Village of Nuts. Why have we come here? It doesn't look like the kind of place people are hanged," he said.

It's not," replied Gustav, "at least not to my knowledge. I have a theory that mandrakes grow wherever human experience has been at its most intense. That might be a place where death has occurred, such as a battlefield, or a site of hangings as you read in my notes this morning, but it might be a place where something good happened."

"So what happened here?" Jan asked.

"The soil is rich, bursting with nut trees, vineyards and orchards. And the exact field we're going to is where a wise woman once lived and loved and healed," Gustav explained. "It's where she came to her end too, which means our mandrake will have been nourished by the bones and blood of a good woman, someone like your mother. While human life ends with burial in earth, plants emerge and draw nourishment from it."

"But what if we dig her up?" Jan asked, thinking of Old Kunigund who'd come with the stars the night he'd been born. "I don't think we should disturb her."

"She'll be at rest far deeper than the root. She won't be disturbed." Gustav looked across the land. "Isn't it peaceful here?"

Jan looked about him. They were surrounded on all sides by groves of hazelnut trees, spindly now and bare, but which in a few months would be dripping with sweet pointed nuts that would be gathered, roasted and ground to make special flour. *Or even brewed into a fertility infusion,* thought Jan, *that's what Mother would have done.*

"Here we are," said Gustav. "We need to head towards the centre of that field," he pointed. "Ludwig!" he called to the driver. "Halt the horses. We'll walk from here."

"As you wish, sir," Ludwig replied. He knew better than to question his master but after overhearing snatches of Jan's conversation about their plans to make a man from a plant he wasn't happy that he or his dog had any part in this. "Folk fiddling with nature," he muttered. "It's nothing but food for the devil."

Still grumbling to himself, Ludwig climbed down from the driver's seat. "Here you go," he said passing Jan his dog's lead. "Look after him, and yourself too. Nothing but trouble comes from meddling."

"Working the land isn't so different from the practice of alchemy," said Gustav as they strode across the field. "Like farmers, alchemists must be mindful of the seasons, of the balance and imbalances of nature, if they are to yield rich harvests.

Here we are," he said, stooping to examine the dark leaves and egg-shaped orange berries of the plant at his feet. "Our Mandragora plant."

He passed Jan the shovel then gave him two clumps of coarse wool. "Put these in your ears and start digging."

The wool felt itchy but Jan knew his ears had to be protected from the sound of the root emerging from the earth. He clouted the shovel onto the ground. Hardened by frost, it seemed impossible to penetrate at first, but he kept on and on until he'd hacked through the topsoil.

"I can see something!" he cried. "I think I've reached the head of the root."

Gustav peered into the trench. "Dig deeper until its lower parts are exposed and then we'll use the dog to uproot it. But we must proceed with haste. The mist is lifting."

Ignoring the ache in his back, Jan dug more and more furiously until he reached the root of the plant.

"Good work," said Gustav. He tied a length of rope to the dog's collar and fastened the other end to the plant's central stalk. "Follow me."

After they'd walked twenty paces Gustav upended the bucket of bloody offal. "Come on, boy," he called. "Breakfast!"

The dog darted towards them, wrenching the root from the earth. Time seemed to stand still as Jan watched it soar upwards, then hover in midair, high as the uppermost branches of the trees, before plunging to the ground.

He ran to it and was alarmed to see it looked even more like a human than the mandrake in the laboratory. About the length of his forearm, it seemed to have the face of a prematurely aged child, at the centre a perfectly formed circle that resembled an open mouth. The roots that twisted from its trunk were flailing arms. The fronds at their tips were grasping fingers.

Gustav wrapped it in a length of sack cloth. "An excellent specimen, and excellent work on your part, Jan. We'll bury it by moonlight tonight."

Back in the cellar of the House of the Seven Stars, Jan laid the mandrake on the workbench and stripped it of its leaves and berries.

"Is this all right?" he asked, holding the naked root aloft.

"Perfect," said Gustav. "Now put it aside. It's time you learned the principles of botany. Follow the tutorial on the intricacies of petal dissection in chapter two," he said, handing Jan Hieronymus Bock's *The Book of Plants*. "Go to the garden if you need fresh specimens."

While Gustav wrote up their findings in his notebook, Jan immersed himself in the book and, once satisfied he understood the instructions, he gathered a selection of flowers and set about studying their structures.

Several hours later, Gustav brought Jan a plate of food.

"Eat," he said. "You must be hungry. But be quick, and change your shirt. We must leave soon."

"Already?" asked Jan, looking up from the magnifying apparatus. "What time is it?"

"Almost midnight. I'll see you outside, quick as you like."

"That's better," said Gustav as Jan appeared in the courtyard, dressed head to toe in black. "We don't want to draw attention to ourselves – not that we're doing anything wrong, of course – but we can't risk having our work disturbed. The mandrake must be uprooted and reburied within a day or else we'll have to start the whole process again. I've left a pail of cow's milk in the garden. Insects will be drawn to it, and so entice the bats we need to infuse it."

He handed Jan the mandrake. "Look after this while I drive. Ludwig's left for the night."

Jan nodded. His mouth was dry, his palms sweaty. Resting on his lap, the wizened root even felt like an infant now. He half expected it to start wriggling and gurgling. As he looked down at the object with a mix of wonder and fear, he remembered Ludwig's caution.

"Why would Ludwig say we were meddling with nature? He said our work was 'food for the devil'."

"Nothing to worry about," Gustav said. "Many a man is

afraid of change and the unknown. We're not meddling; we're deciphering the wonders of nature for the good of humankind."

Jan sat back, chewing his lower lip. Gustav was right. While he'd been thrilled by the miracles he'd witnessed in the laboratory – the twitches of life in the butterfly, the miniaturisation of a peahen – the thought of how their discoveries might be applied was what really excited him.

After a short journey through the city, its streets deserted but for the occasional dog scavenging outside a closed inn for scraps of food, and vagrants searching for shelter, Gustav heaved the horses to a standstill. They tied the horses' reins to a fence and trekked along the lane. Still cradling the mandrake, Jan paused at the cemetery gates. As he peered inside, eyes moving from headstone to headstone, he thought of all the people at rest here, and of those they'd left behind. He noticed a freshly dug mound of earth to the right and, wondering whose grave this would fill come the morning, and what had caused their death, he took a deep breath and followed Gustav inside.

With only the moonlight to see by, they left the central path which split the burial ground in two and fought their way through thickets to the far edge of the cemetery, away from the graves. Jan could see his breath before him, but little else. They were now deep among twisted trees and brambles and all was still, until a streak of light flashed close by them. Jan froze, held his breath as a rush of wind whirled above them, causing the spiky silhouettes of leafless branches to prod the air like wizened fingers. The light came nearer. With pounding heart, Jan raised his hands to his eyes. He peeped through his fingers, saw the white chest of a fox cub and gave a nervous gasp of relief. Nothing to be afraid of. The animal stopped in its tracks and stared at them with glassy black and bronze eyes. Then, with a swish of its red tail, it vanished into the undergrowth.

"Here's a good place," Gustav said. "The hedge will protect it."

Jan dug a hole, laid down the root and covered it with earth, all the while fighting the thought that he was burying a living being.

"Well done," said Gustav. "You've excelled yourself today. You've made me proud. But brace yourself for the weeks for come. Preparing the bat-infused milk and coming here to feed the mandrake for the next month will be hard work, but I promise this will be more than worth the effort. You reap what you sow."

Jan felt a surge of satisfaction. He was glad they'd be home soon, in warm beds, away from this place of death and thorns, but he knew that until now he wouldn't have been able to enter a graveyard. He hadn't been near one since the morning he'd buried his parents, so tonight he'd proved he could rise above his fears. He also knew that something else had changed. He felt close to his uncle. He knew their work together had given him everything to strive for.

They hadn't gone more than a few paces when Jan sensed something behind him. He glanced over his shoulder, expecting to see another fox. Nothing but the jabbing branches and crooked headstones. But while reason told him he had nothing to fear, still Jan felt he was being scrutinised, as if the glistening gems of frost on the leaves were tiny staring eyes.

A crow cawed overhead. Jan looked up at the star-speckled sky. Was it their dazzling gaze he could feel? Or was it the breath of the plague ogre? Or was it nothing at all?

Chapter Five
Enchantress of Eggs

Greta pulled her ermine stole close and nuzzled her chin into the soft fur, for the night was bitter and her bones cold. She'd seen the carriage leave the courtyard and swerve onto the Lane of the Light of the Moon.

Where are they going? she wondered, as she moved from the window to her dressing table to check on her bird. She'd passed her day with no company but for the peahen, which had laid its first egg that morning.

"Gustav?" she called into the darkness of the hallway. "Jan?"

As expected, no answer had come, so she flitted to the cellar, birdcage swaying from her arm. She turned the iron handle. In his haste to leave, Jan had left the laboratory unlocked. Greta peered into the room and gasped.

She saw the glasshouse of birds, the bottled specimens of embryos, the shelves of bones and preserved reptiles. She found the Milkwood Monarch butterflies and pressed her nose to the glass, watching the creatures feed from the flowering milkwood plants. She saw how their flickering wings kept colliding with the case. And she fought an urge to slide open the lid to release them, for she knew that though they were pretty, they were deadly poisonous.

Having no idea how much longer Gustav would be, and not wishing to be discovered, Greta forced herself from the butterflies, for she wanted to see the life-generating liquid Jan had spoken of. She checked the shelves, opened cabinet after cabinet, case after case. She worked methodically, unruffled by the scale of the task, even though time was against her. Then, after a while, her meticulousness paid off when she opened a drawer beneath the workbench and saw a row of jars. The thick fluid they held matched Jan's description of the elixir. *Might this be it?* She took one and, heartbeat quickening, she read the label, closely examined its contents. Yes! she said, taking an empty bottle and decanting only a few drops lest Gustav would realise it was missing.

Now desperate to uncover more of their secrets, Greta leafed through the documents spread across the bench. "'Methods of Homunculi Creation,'" she read aloud. "Incredible!"

She read on and learned how the blood of the hanged could be used to create semi-human creatures, that mandrake berries might incite love. And she learned how freshly dug mandrake roots can be reburied in graveyards and nurtured to create new life.

As she thumbed through Gustav's papers an idea came to her. "Why should I wait for him to reveal his magic to the world? Perhaps I could make my own creature. I could use your egg, couldn't I?" she addressed her bird. "I could replace the egg of the black hen with your treasure. If nothing happens, no matter. But if it works ... who knows?"

Greta coaxed her peahen from the cage and picked up the warm egg. She pierced it with a needle and poured out a small amount of foetal fluid, and though this was her first attempt at anything of this nature, she had the firm hand and poise of a professional.

Next she pricked her forefinger and dripped the blood into the egg, along with a drop of the elixir and a lock of her hair. Rather than resealing it with wax, as the notes specified, she snipped the end from one of her bird's feathers — a single indigo and emerald eye — and secured it over the hole with more blood. Finally, she placed it in a nutshell she'd found on one of the shelves.

"To keep you extra safe. But what now?"

> Bury the egg in dung on the first day of the lunar cycle. Once it's had time to form — in thirty or forty days — a miniature human will emerge from the egg.
>
> Feed the creature lavender seeds and earthworms and it will obey and protect.
>
> **WARNING:** failure to care for the creature and feed it this diet may result in it turning on its creator.

"I think we're ready," she said, cradling her creation. Then she went to the garden and buried it among her roses. She began to chant in a soft, low voice.

> Your shell is earth, your white is water
> Your membrane is air, your yolk is fire, and gold:
> The heart of everything.
> Your whole is as heaven
> Protecting life, cultivating immortality.

Just then, the moon emerged from the clouds and, swathed in its brilliant light, Greta returned to her chambers. As she concealed the bottle of serum in a drawer, her bird gave a shrill cry. It had laid two more eggs.

"A sign!" she cried, freeing the creature from its cage. It stepped into the golden glow of the candles. "Let me tell you a story, my beauty."

The Nine Peahens and the Golden Apples

There was once a king whose palace was set in a magnificent garden. And at the centre of this garden was a tree that sprouted a fresh crop of golden apples each day. By morning the tree flowered and bore fruit and by evening the fruit ripened, but none of the golden apples ever survived to the next day.

One day the king called his eldest son to him and said, "Son, tonight you will sit watch in my garden to discover who's stealing my golden apples. If you are successful, I shall give you half my kingdom."

The king's eldest son accepted his father's challenge and that same night he went to the garden, armed with a sword and a crossbow for protection, and sat beneath the apple tree. But he hadn't been there long when he was overcome with drowsiness. His arms dropped to his sides, his eyes closed and he slipped into a deep sleep. When he woke at dawn the apples were gone.

"Did you see the thief?" asked the king next morning.

"No," replied the prince, shaking his head. "There was no thief. The apples disappeared of their own accord."

"Nonsense," barked the king. "How can that be?" So he ordered his second-born son to keep watch and catch the thief that night.

The second prince armed himself as his older brother had done and spent the night beneath the tree of golden apples. But he too was overcome with a desire to sleep and when he woke at dawn the apples were gone.

Next morning, the king went to the tree. "Did you see the thief?" he asked.

"There was no thief," replied the second-born son. "The apples disappeared of their own accord. But I found this," he said, proffering a single peahen feather that shimmered with specks of golden light.

"Tsk!" said the king, tossing the feather aside. "The thief must be found!"

"I'd like to try, Father," said the king's youngest son.

"You?" laughed the king. "My son, you are small and not yet wise enough to undertake such a task. If your older brothers have failed, how will you succeed?"

But the youngest son was a determined boy. "Please allow me to try," he pleaded. "I promise I won't let you down."

"Very well," agreed the king. "But promise me nothing. Don't be surprised if you're unsuccessful."

At nightfall, the youngest son did as his older brothers had done. He took a sword and crossbow to the tree, but he also brought the skin of a hedgehog to lay on his lap so if he fell asleep and his arms dropped down, he would be woken by its prickles.

Shortly before midnight the youngest prince began to feel sleepy. His eyes closed, his head drooped and his hands fell. "Ouch!" he cried as the hedgehog skin prickled his hands. He looked up and, to his relief, saw that the palace garden was still bathed in the golden light of apples. Not a single one had been taken. Then something caught his eye; a formation of birds soaring towards the palace. As they neared him, the young prince counted nine golden plumed peahens.

Eight of the birds alighted in the tree while the ninth landed next to the prince and transformed itself into a beautiful girl whose hair gleamed like spun gold, whose cheeks were as rosy as apples and whose eyes were as blue as a deep, deep lake.

The young prince and the enchanting girl talked together while the peahens gathered the golden apples, and the prince learned that they took them not out of greed or malice, but because they depended on them for nourishment. Once all the apples had been collected, the girl thanked the prince for the pleasure of his company and turned to go.

Captivated by her grace and beauty, the prince begged the bird-girl to stay, but she had to leave. So she gave him two apples – one for him, the second for his father – before transforming herself back into a peahen and taking flight with her eight companions.

Next morning the young prince delighted his father with a gift of two golden apples and that night he returned to the tree and the same thing happened, and again the next night, and the next until, on the seventh night, his jealous older brothers decided to bribe an old woman to spy on him.

At dusk the old woman hid herself beneath the tree and waited. At midnight the nine peahens came and again the ninth became a beautiful girl. The old woman reached up and snipped off one of the girl's golden curls to show the king's eldest sons. All at once the girl became a peahen and she and her eight companions took flight.

The young prince jumped up and cried out, "Come back, sweet enchantress!" But she was gone so he ordered the old woman to be tied to a horse's tail and dragged through the streets as punishment for frightening his love away.

by

The next night the peahens didn't come, nor the next, nor the next so the young prince left his father's palace to search for the beautiful girl, taking only one servant with him. After a few days he came to a castle on the edge of a lake, home to an elderly queen and her daughter. The prince went to the castle and asked if the queen knew of the nine golden peahens.

"I do," replied the queen. "They come every day at noon to bathe in the lake. But you should let them alone. Here, meet my daughter. Is she not pretty? Is she not gentle and kind-hearted? If you marry her, all my wealth will be yours."

But the prince had no interest in the queen's daughter, nor her wealth. He went directly to the lake, thinking only of the ninth peahen that transformed itself into the most beautiful girl he'd ever seen. However, the old queen was a sharp-witted woman and knew the prince would go to the lake, so she bribed his servant to betray his master with the promise of a bag of gold coins.

"Take these enchanted bellows," she ordered. "Use them to blow soothing air onto your master's neck. He will be put into a sleep as deep as death, and unable to speak to the peahens."

The servant did as the queen commanded and by the time the nine peahens came the prince had been lulled into a sleep as deep as death by the enchanted bellows.

Suffused in light that reflected in the lake and turned its still waters to liquid gold, eight of the peahens went to bathe while the ninth transformed into the enchantress and went to the young prince.

"Awaken, my love!" she called. "I thought I'd never see you again!"

But no matter how hard she tried, the girl couldn't wake the prince, so she became a bird and the nine peahens flew away.

After some time, the young prince woke and asked his servant if the birds had come. When he learned they had, he flew into a rage but returned to the lake the next day. Once again the servant blew the enchanted bellows and his master fell into a sleep as deep as death.

When the peahens came the beautiful girl tried to wake him but her cries went unheard, her caresses unfelt. "It's as if he were dead!" she lamented. She turned to the unscrupulous servant. "Tell your master I shall return tomorrow but never again after that," and with that she and her companions flew away.

When the prince woke the servant told him what the girl had said and he flew into an even greater rage. "Why didn't you wake me?" he roared.

The next day the prince trotted his horse around the lake while he waited for the birds to come, thinking this would keep him alert. But the servant also took a horse and blew the bellows on his master's neck from behind as they rode. Sure enough, the prince began to feel drowsy. His hands became limp, he dropped the reins and slipped from the horse onto the silty banks of the lake just as the peahens appeared.

The sight of the young prince asleep again filled the beautiful bird girl with woe, but she said to the servant, "Tell your master if he wants to find me, he should seek the wandering old man in the depths of a far-off land, for I shall never return to this place."

66

When the prince awoke and heard what had happened he took his sword and sliced off his servant's head, certain he'd been betrayed by him. Then he left the palace by the lake and went in search of the old man who might lead him to his love.

After some months travelling alone through unfamiliar lands, the young prince met an old hermit wandering through the woods. "Do you know of the nine golden peahens?" he asked.

"Indeed I do," answered the wanderer. "Walk on until you come to a large gate. Pass through the gate on the right hand side until you come to the City of Peahens and there you will find the palace of the nine birds you seek."

The young prince did as the hermit said and he soon came to the City of Peahens. It was like nowhere he'd seen. The houses were nests on stilts, woven from golden twigs. Instead of flowers and trees the gardens were adorned with feathers.

And in place of the sky was a gleaming golden dome that encased the entire city.

As he took all this in, the young prince understood why the nine birds had come to take his father's apples. There was no fruit here, no grain. There seemed to be nothing to eat.

"Behold, the Queen!" boomed a voice from the palace. The queen emerged and the young prince saw it was the beautiful enchantress he'd been seeking.

"At last we can be together!" he cried.

"Yes, we can," she smiled, but then her beautiful face became sad. Tears fell from her deep blue eyes and rolled down her rosy red cheeks. "You may remain here as my husband and King of the City of Peahens, but to do so will mean renouncing your humanity and becoming a bird. Or you may leave now as a man and remain a man until the day of your death, but you will never see me again."

The young prince was overcome with anguish. "How can this be?" he cried, as he raged around the palace courtyard, wondering if he could exist as a bird in a city without food, wondering if he could live without ever seeing the beautiful girl again.

Then he heard a creaking sound. He looked up and saw the city gates were closing behind him. He hadn't noticed he'd stepped outside the threshold. The decision had been made.

From beyond the city gates the young prince saw the enchantress transform into a bird, rise to the top of the golden dome and gather the whole city in the expanse of her wings. Everything shone so bright that the young prince was forced to shield his eyes. When he opened them it was as if the city and the birds and his beloved enchantress had never existed. All that remained was a single golden feather.

"And that was the story of The Nine Peahens and the Golden Apples," Greta yawned. "You'll never vanish like the enchantress, will you?" she said to her bird. "You and I shall be as *one* enchantress."

Chapter Six

In the Depths of the Dancing Water

By Saturday morning Greta's peahen had laid six eggs, each encased in a mushroom-white shell, dappled with dozens of tawny dots. She woke to find her bird nuzzling the two that had appeared overnight.

"Well done," she praised it, proffering a palm of seeds. "So many in only five days."

Picking up the cage, she swept to the kitchen, hair arranged high on her head like an ebony crown, feet shielded by scarlet slippers, shoulders shrouded in a crimson cape, for though the morning was fair, Greta rarely felt warm.

"Good morning, Jan."

He jumped, almost dropping the bread he was about to sink his teeth into. "Aunt Greta! I didn't hear you."

"A tread more delicate than air," she said placing the birdcage on the table. "I've scarcely seen either of you for days. I suppose you must be absorbed in something of importance."

"You're right. It's the new experiment we've begun," Jan

explained. "We have to visit the graveyard every morning to feed the mandrake root we buried there. Gustav thinks we can create a kind of living creature from it. We'll test the elixir on it once it's been animated."

"I see," Greta replied. "I've heard of such experiments. And do you think you'll succeed?"

"Don't worry," said Jan. "Gustav knows what he's doing. We both do."

"I'm not worried. Far from it."

"How do you like your bird?" asked Jan, peering into the cage.

"She's the perfect companion," said Greta. "And fertile, too. She's laid half a dozen eggs already."

"That's incredible. Does Gustav know? He said peahens normally only lay ten in a lifetime but, of course, this is no ordinary bird." Jan reached out to touch an egg through the gilded bars.

"Don't," said Greta, taking hold of Jan's wrist. "She's very protective of them."

Just then, the maid came from the pantry carrying one of the rabbits that had been hanging there.

"I'll do that, Alzbeth," she said, taking the dead animal from the girl.

"As you wish, Mistress."

Greta laid out the rabbit, selected the sharpest knife and cut a neat slit from its throat all the way down its white belly.

As he watched her slip the blade beneath the skin to loosen it, then deftly peel off its pelt, Jan found himself wondering what went on in her mind.

"You're very skilled with the knife," he said. "Gustav would say you have a surgeon's precision, but why don't you let Alzbeth do it?"

"Because I find it gratifying, but also to remind me that

I'm still a servant myself, and so shall I be until my will is entirely my own. When that day comes someone else shall do the skinning. There," she announced. "Ready to be portioned and prepared for roasting."

"Jan!" Gustav's voice came from the hallway. "Work beckons!"

"I should go," said Jan. "Will you be all right?" he asked. Her words had unnerved him. What did she mean that she was still a servant?

"Of course. You shouldn't keep Gustav waiting. I'm sure I'll find something to occupy me."

Gustav and Jan went to the courtyard to check the pail. And there they found the bodies of three bats, stiffened by death and frost, wings tucked tight against their chests.

"Three!" said Jan. "That's good, isn't it? The most we've had yet."

"Healthy specimens, too," Gustav replied. "They'll have nourished the milk well. You know the procedure. Remove them and pick up the pail. Ludwig's waiting. Careful you don't spill any. Our mandrake man mustn't go thirsty."

———————

They left Ludwig outside the graveyard gates and moved through the morning mist, boots crunching on the frost-hardened grass until they came to the place they'd buried the root. Then Jan poured out the pail and stood there, staring down at the milk-moistened patch.

"What's on your mind?" asked Gustav.

Jan scratched his eyelid. "I was thinking of what will happen when we un-earth it, when we've dried it in an oven with some verbena."

"We still have a few more weeks of watering. Then we shall test its resistance to different diseases. We shall see how it fares after being fed different potencies of the Dancing Water. If he survives, if he withstands the infections, the signs are good that the elixir will work on humans. But remember," Gustav continued, "homunculi will turn on their creators if they're not given the utmost respect."

"I remember," said Jan. "I'll treat it well." He paused, jerked his head to the left, then the right. "Did you hear that? There's someone here. In the trees."

"Don't let the graveyard get to you. The dead can do no harm. It's the living you have to watch. I imagine it's another fox. Come," Gustav said, patting Jan's shoulder. "Our work here is done for today."

Jan picked up the pail and followed Gustav to the carriage, all the while glancing around him. But he saw nothing.

***

And so the weeks passed. Jan and Gustav would visit the graveyard each day to feed the root. Then they'd return to the laboratory to monitor the butterflies and develop new strains of the elixir. And as these weeks passed, Jan was filled with a sense of change. Partly because each morning he'd go to his window and see shoots of new leaves sprouting from branches. But the difference Jan felt was more than the seasonal spinning of nature's wheel. Jan sensed change in himself, and Gustav noticed it too.

Day by day, he grew more and more impressed with his nephew's progress. He believed young scholars should make their own discoveries and mistakes, draw their own conclusions, so while he remained on hand to offer guidance, Gustav allowed Jan to experiment freely. He was overjoyed to see how his nephew was growing up. He spoke more confidently, he held himself taller and, one day, he revealed something that made Gustav prouder than he'd thought possible.

"May I ask you something?" said Jan, his eyes sparkling. "I think I'd like to become a doctor one day. I mean, I *know* I want to become a doctor."

"Of course, you're able," Gustav said. "There's no question of that."

Jan went to the workbench and unveiled his latest work. He knew ingredients exemplifying the four elements had to form the base of the elixir, so he'd constructed an arrangement of apparatus to distil its basic elemental components. Jars of clear liquids linked by a series of glass tubes bubbled on frames above candles. Dead insects, finely ground into coloured powders of red, yellow and green smouldered on dishes in small clay table-top ovens.

"Have you had any success with this new mixture?" asked Gustav.

"It revived a dying beetle this morning," said Jan, "but only briefly so I've introduced some new ingredients. A sprinkle of salt crushed with clay to strengthen the element of earth, and a purifying drop of lemon balm. I'll leave a bottle to settle overnight and try it on another insect in the morning."

"Excellent. It may even be ready by the time we uproot the mandrake. Make sure you lock it away. You can't risk it being contaminated. And be sure not to mix up the old and new versions. Keep them separate."

"Of course," said Jan. "I lock the latest sample in this cabinet, and all my previous efforts are in the drawer."

"Supper will be served shortly, if you have time to dine this evening," said Greta who, unseen and unheard, had slipped into the room behind them.

"Didn't you think to knock?" asked Gustav. "We might have been at a crucial point."

"And are you?" she asked, walking to the workbench.

"What's all this?"

"Distillation equipment for our serum," explained Jan. "It's developing well. It might even be ready by the time we uproot the mandrake next week."

"And to think I've done little more than prune a few plants in my garden while you've been perfecting a life-generating elixir. Tell me, how are your other experiments going? What about the butterflies? Are they still poisonous? Have they been weaned from their diet of milkwood?"

"Not yet," said Jan, locking away his latest serum sample. "But soon, we hope."

"I see," Greta replied. "Then I shall leave you to it." She departed the cellar as silently as she had appeared there.

Gustav gazed through the glass case. "I'm sure there were more here last time I looked. Might I have miscounted?"

"I don't think so," Jan shrugged. "But it's hard to say. They move so fast. Do you really think we're so close to success?"

"No," said Gustav, "We're not, but you are. This is all your doing. I merely set you off on the path to success. You've made your own way along it, chosen which turnings to take."

"No. It's our path, and we travel it together," Jan insisted. "Shall we go upstairs? I'm famished."

"You keep Greta company this evening. I feel incredibly drowsy. I'm sure a good sleep will see me right. Don't forget to leave the pail in the courtyard." He reached out and gripped Jan's arm. "Goodnight, son. Make sure you get plenty of rest too, so we're both ready to take a few more steps down that path tomorrow, eh?"

"I will," said Jan. "Sleep well."

Once everyone had retired for the night and the House of the Seven Stars had fallen silent as the dead, Greta stole to her garden. She went to the place she'd buried her nut-encased egg, sprinkled the area with fresh rosewater and watched the clear liquid seep through the dark soil. She knew the instructions had specified feeding it lavender and earthworms, but she'd thought rosewater more appropriate sustenance for a creature of her making.

The shell and the earth.
The white and the water.
The membrane and air.
The yolk and the fire.
The golden heart of the world.

Soft and slow, she breathed these words, over and over, until the moon vanished behind a passing cloud. Then she reached out and plucked a rosebud from a bush. A thorn scratched her finger. *No petals without thorns. No beauty without pain.*

Chapter Seven
Ogre's Return

When Jan opened his eyes next morning the position of the sun told him it was already late. He checked his pocket watch; it was after ten. "I don't believe it," he grumbled, pulling on his clothes and dragging a comb through his hair. But when he went downstairs, the house was quiet, and cold. No fires had been lit, no breakfast prepared.

Jan scrambled to the laboratory, bootlaces still undone, but that, too, was silent and empty. "Uncle can't have gone to the graveyard without me," he groaned.

"He-*llo*!" he called, racing back upstairs. As he went to check Gustav's room, Greta appeared at his side.

"Don't," she said, laying a hand on his as he reached for the door handle. "Don't go in."

"Why not?"

"He's gone," she whispered.

"I knew it! Why didn't he wake me? When did he leave?"

"No, Jan. He's *gone*."

Then, as he stared into Greta's stony grey eyes, Jan felt that twist in the pit of his stomach that told him something was wrong.

"No ..." he said, shaking his head as he pushed past her. "No."

But yes.

There, on the other side of the door, was his Uncle Gustav, laid out on the bed, arms folded across his chest, eyes shut fast. He looked almost as if he were in a deep sleep but there was something different about his face. It had lost its life, become a mask. And, as Jan stared harder, he saw something else. He saw terror and shock. The expression of a man who'd died in the throes of agony.

He looked from Gustav to Greta. She too was staring at the corpse, as if she'd been drained of life and blood herself.

"It can't be true. It's *not* true," he cried. "He wasn't ill. I won't believe it."

"You must," said Greta. "We've lost him. He's dead."

Her words pierced Jan's heart like shards of ice. He staggered to the bed, fell to his knees. He laid his head on Gustav's chest. "Wake up," he pleaded. "Wake up!"

"Come away," said Greta, tugging his shoulder. "Let him be at rest."

"The serum!" called Jan, stumbling to the door and knocking into a chair. In the commotion, a solitary butterfly emerged from behind the drawn curtains and fluttered around Jan's head. He swiped it away.

"Calm yourself," Greta ordered, grasping his arm.

Jan wasn't listening. He freed himself from Greta's grip and raced to the cellar to fetch the elixir, but collapsed outside the laboratory door. "If it can't even keep a beetle alive, what use is it to Uncle Gustav?"

Greta went to him. "You must be strong. You must behave as your uncle would expect; with dignity and strength."

"But why did he ... how can he be ...? There was nothing wrong with him. He mentioned feeling tired, but nothing more. How is it possible? What will we do without him? What will we do?"

"You're made of strong stuff. You survived losing your parents, didn't you? You keep their memory alive, and so you shall Gustav's."

Jan picked himself up. "Yes," he said. "I shall."

Jan was sitting on the edge of his bed, stomach churning, head pounding. It was the morning of Gustav's internment and he didn't want to leave his room. The very thought of it terrified him, for it meant having to say goodbye to Gustav forever. Memories of his parents' funeral came flooding back and Jan felt as if he was drowning. He'd only just begun getting to know his uncle who, in so little time, had given Jan faith in his abilities, and hope for the future. But now all that seemed lost.

"It's time," Greta called from the foot of the stairs.

He stood, took a deep breath. "I miss you," he said, catching sight of his reflection in the mirror. "All of you."

"Ready to leave, Mistress?" asked Ludwig.

"We are," Greta replied, gazing ahead at nothing.

I'm not ready, thought Jan, choking back his tears. *How could anyone ever be ready for this?*

Gustav's coffin was borne by six men wearing black masks and hooded robes, as was the custom, its passage through the burial ground guided by glowing torches.

Dressed in a long black gown, its bodice embroidered with beads of jet and onyx, Greta headed the procession of

mourners, with Jan at her side. She looked at him through her sheer veil. But he couldn't respond. He felt numb, separated from himself and everything around him. He could see the coffin just ahead of him. He could see the moon above him and his aunt to his left. He knew there were birds in the trees, worms in the earth and stars in the sky, but it was as if they didn't exist. It was as if the world had stopped: he no longer felt part of it.

The same words kept beating through his head, over and over. *It's our path, and we travel it together. It's our path, and we travel it together. It's our path, and we travel it together.* But Jan knew he'd have to travel their path alone from now on. As he stood over the grave while the minister committed Gustav's body, he wished the earth would swallow him up too, so the pain would end, so the ogre couldn't find him and come for his loved ones a third time.

Once the mourners had left, Jan went alone to the place he and Gustav had buried their mandrake. As he knelt there, imagining the fronds of the mandrake's fingers emerging from the earth, Gustav's voice came to him, as strong and clear as if he were standing behind him. *While human life ends with burial in earth, plants emerge and draw nourishment from it.*

Jan set off home, dreading the fact that his uncle wouldn't be there. He kept walking, so numbed by grief he scarcely noticed it had started to snow. A flash of winter in this most chilling of springtimes.

Jan forced himself to keep busy in the long days that followed. He continued to adapt the serum, adding more lemon balm, further refining the soil and the salt, all the while listening for Gustav's voice. And it came, offering encouragement and advice, and so Jan felt Gustav lived on through the work they'd begun, and the progress he made.

As these days passed, he also assumed responsibility for running the household, stepping into his uncle's shoes as best he could. He made sure Ludwig and Alzbeth saw to all their duties, and he made sure bills were settled in good time.

But Greta wasn't happy with this. "I'll manage our domestic and financial affairs," she'd insisted.

While Jan had protested, thinking that as the man of the house he should take responsibility for such matters, secretly he was glad he could concentrate on his science. "Very well," he agreed. "If you don't mind, I shall go to the graveyard this afternoon. Our mandrake is due to be dug up. I shall visit Uncle's grave while I'm there."

"Take your time," said Greta. "I have my own matters to attend to today."

After a solitary lunch, Jan went to the graveyard alone. He crouched at Gustav's grave and wept awhile, for he'd forced himself to stifle his tears at home. Greta found it too painful. He was worried about her. He'd hardly seen her leave her chambers since the funeral. She'd withdrawn even further from the real world, had moved deeper into her universe in the eaves.

Jan walked on towards the place they'd buried the mandrake. As it came into view, his blood ran cold. He could see a heap of earth and, beside it, the hole was empty. He took a rock and stabbed it into the soil, desperately hoping the root might be there somewhere. After burrowing deep and wide around the hole, it was still nowhere to be found.

Jan was beside himself with despair, and anger. He knew he could return to Nussdorf, find another mandrake and start the experiment again. But that wasn't the point. He wanted this mandrake, the one he and Gustav had worked on together. Then he was struck by a thought: had someone really been there, watching his every move, the night they'd buried it? Waiting for an opportunity to steal it? But perhaps his imagination was getting the better of him, perhaps an animal had taken it. There was no way of knowing and the fact remained that the mandrake had gone.

"I won't fail you with the elixir," he said out loud. "I promise. I'll never let that out of my sight. I shall keep working until it's able to heal all ills."

But there were more surprises to come that evening. When Jan turned onto the Lane of the Light of the Moon he saw the carriage laden with trunks and chests. He ran the rest of the way.

"What's all this?" he called to Ludwig who was adjusting the horses' tack. "Are you going somewhere?"

"You'd better ask the mistress. My business is neither to question, nor to answer questions. Last I saw she was digging around in her rose garden."

Jan dashed inside and saw that the walls had been stripped of their paintings and tapestries, the cabinets emptied of ornaments, the furniture covered with sheets. "Greta?"

He eventually found her in the laboratory, bent over the workbench drawer. He was shocked to see she'd abandoned her sombre mourning outfit for an elaborate turquoise gown. It was customary for a lady to wear black for several months after being widowed.

"What's happening?" he asked, still panting. "Where is everything?"

"I wasn't expecting you so soon," Greta replied. "I ... I wanted to spend some last moments down here, among everything Gustav held so dear."

"Why ... why are you dressed like that?"

Greta lowered her eyes. "To help shed my sorrow. Gustav wouldn't want our lives to be filled with gloom, would he?"

"But why is everything packed up?"

"I wanted to surprise you. I'd hoped to have everything ready before your return," she said, picking up her birdcage. "I can't stay here surrounded by Gustav's ghost. I'm going to Prague. I think his Elixir of Life should be brought before the Emperor."

"What do you mean?" asked Jan, wondering how she intended to do that. Only he and Gustav knew anything about the elixir. "I don't understand. When did you decide this?"

"Opportunities must be seized when they arise," she replied, "and I intend to grasp mine now. I realise this must come as quite a shock so, please, don't feel you have to accompany me. I'd understand if you'd prefer to return to your village. I know how you miss it."

A thousand thoughts flashed through Jan's mind. This was so sudden, so unexpected. It was almost as if Greta didn't want him to come with her. He asked himself if he did want to return to his village, but realised there was nothing for him there now. His parents existed in his thoughts and heart, not a physical place. And since working with Gustav he'd glimpsed a new world of possibilities he couldn't turn his back on.

Jan didn't understand Greta's behaviour. She seemed calm and assured, but her actions were irrational. So little time had passed since Gustav's death. It didn't seem right – it didn't seem normal – for one so recently widowed to put herself through further turmoil.

"No. I'll come with you. I won't let you go alone. I'll find someone in Prague to take me on as their apprentice. I'll work on the elixir there. You said it was the City of Alchemy."

"And gold," Greta reminded him. "If you're worried about the elixir, you could leave it with me. I'll see it remains in good hands."

"I must develop it myself," Jan insisted. "I promised. I'm coming with you. But what about all the birds and creatures in uncle's garden?"

"They've been taken care of."

"What do you mean?"

"I set them free."

"Not the Milkwood Monarchs, I hope?" Jan gasped. "They're dangerous. They shouldn't be let loose."

He ran to the case. It was empty. "Where are they?"

"Destroyed."

A knock came at the door. It was Ludwig. "I've prepared the horses, Mistress."

"Will you stay in Prague with us?" asked Jan. "And your dog?"

"Perhaps. There's nothing to keep me here. Dog's dead. Found him in the garden this afternoon. Eyes wide open like he'd seen the devil."

"*Dead?* What happened? He wasn't sick, was he?"

"Neither was the master." Ludwig replied. "There's no telling what can happen when the devil's afoot."

"That's enough of your nonsense, Ludwig," Greta chastised. "Don't you think we've had enough upset of late?" She turned to Jan. "We have a long journey ahead. If you're certain you want to come, go and pack a few things. I shall see you in the carriage."

In a dream, Jan gathered Gustav's notebooks and doctor's robes, unlocked his latest serum samples from their cabinet. Then he stood there awhile, in the centre of the Cellar of Science, taking everything in, painting a picture he hoped he'd remember forever. The chequered floor Gustav had paced, his sable fur-collared coat draped over an armchair. The shelves of books they'd read together; the diagrams of butterflies they'd studied. The stuffed animals, preserved reptiles, exotic eggs and bleached bones. A lifetime's passion, a world of knowledge, a universe of possibilities.

THE SECOND CHAMBER

Scientifica

Chapter Eight
At the House of the Hidden

Prague, Bohemia

J an didn't sleep that first night of their journey. He was too
confused and anxious about what might lie ahead. He
wondered what Gustav would make of them leaving like
this. How would he feel about him deserting the cellar,
and Greta discarding her mourning clothes so soon? But Jan
knew it was pointless to ponder the rights and wrongs of
Greta's decision, for the decision had been made and they
were on their way to a foreign city. He would just have to
make the best of things, for all their sakes. He tried to turn
his attention to more practical matters, like where they'd live,
and what they'd do, and how he'd continue his work when
they arrived.

"Do you know anyone in Prague?" he'd asked Greta as the
carriage turned off the Lane of the Light of the Moon.

"Please, Jan. I need peace. Try to rest," she'd pleaded. "We
have days of travel ahead."

So he sat back in his seat, watching the grey drape of dusk
blanket the city, asking himself if these might be his last

glimpses of so many landmarks he'd come to know: the Hofburg Palace, the Graben Street vegetable stalls, the church of St Peter, the cathedral of St Stephen. All the lanes and alleys and parks he'd explored. Then, as they clattered through Vienna's outskirts, Gustav's final resting place. Jan promised himself he'd remain true to all his uncle had taught him, no matter what lay ahead.

On they drove, through the night and still Jan didn't sleep. And though it was dark, he sensed the landscape change as they left the city and went deeper into the countryside. The air was colder, the tracks rougher, the night blacker. He wrapped himself in a blanket and stared into the darkness, imagining the villages and hamlets they passed through, the people who lived in them, the lives they led.

He was still awake at dawn. He saw the sky lighten from indigo to blue. He watched the sun rise over the fields and meadows of the Austrian countryside, and then it began to snow, thick and fast. Ludwig pulled the horses to a halt when they came to the next village, for the path was beginning to merge with the fields. It wasn't safe to travel, especially as both he and the horses were exhausted.

"Fetch yourselves some food," said Greta. "I'll stay here, with the luggage."

Jan and Ludwig trudged through the snow and found a tavern that served bread and smoked meats, and though Jan didn't feel hungry he forced something down then listened to Ludwig debate the best route from the village to Prague. Once the snowstorm had passed they returned to Greta and continued on their way, and by sunset they'd crossed into Moravia through the hilly town of Mikulov.

Jan slipped in and out of sleep for the remainder of the journey. His rest was disturbed by the jolts and jerks of the carriage as they crossed choppy streams and rattled over rough tracks, and also by nightmares. Then he'd stir to find the eyes he'd felt burning into him belonged not to the Ogre, but to Greta.

"Go back to sleep, Jan," she'd say, averting her stare. "There's nothing to fear. It's only a dream."

He'd drift off again, and sometimes happier thoughts came to him; memories of his parents alive and happy, visions of his future scientific success, but he'd wake to remember that his mother and father and uncle really were dead, and realise that each spin of the carriage wheels was taking him further from the House of the Seven Stars, the place he'd come to call home.

And so the days rolled on, and so the nights passed, and Jan wished all this upset and uncertainty would end – really end – and that he could lie down in a bed and sleep through his grief, untroubled by dreams or nightmares or Greta's gaze.

Then, at last, Ludwig pulled the horses to a standstill outside a house called The Three Ostriches.

Jan rubbed his eyes, half wondering if he might still be dreaming, for everything around him seemed a whirl of madness. But this was real: they'd arrived in time to witness Emperor Rudolf's procession marking the return of Imperial power to Prague.

The streets thronged with people of every age and class, all made merry by jesters and tumblers somersaulting to the discordant melodies of parading musicians. It was overwhelming after the austerity of their journey, and Jan struggled to keep his balance as he left the carriage, still clutching the sack that held his serum and books. He looked beyond the immediate mayhem and saw that the city was enclosed within a circle of hills, that spires and turrets speared the sky in every direction.

"Is that the castle?" he asked, shielding his eyes from the

sun as he pointed up at St Vitus's Cathedral.

"It must be," Greta replied. "Imagine the riches that lie beyond those walls. A secret city within a city of secrets. What I wouldn't give to venture inside."

The peahen gave a shrill chirrup and fanned out its tail. "And you will come too, my beauty!"

Jan and Greta fought their way through the crowds and found a spot on the Charles Bridge, the link between the Castle District and Lesser Quarter of the west and the Old Town, Josefov Ghetto and New Town in the east. The waters of the Vltava River below were turbulent and thick slabs of ice had formed on its silty banks. Jan leaned over the bridge, exhilarated by the sensation of the wind whipping his cheeks.

Suddenly, the crowd thrust forward.

Jan peered over the heads of the people before him and saw the procession approach, a slow-moving cavalcade headed by the Emperor. In golden robes, Rudolf personified the sun; both were, in their own ways, celestial forces around which the world revolved. To the right of his carriage was a courtier leading his beloved lion on a chain. Directly behind were his brothers, the Archdukes Matthias and Ernst, then Katerina, his mistress, and their six children: five boys and their sister, who stood apart from them, accompanied by her lady-in-waiting. They were all masked and dressed as Roman gods and goddesses. At the rear came Rudolf's closest confidantes – his chief political advisors and physicians, astrologers and artists – resplendent in costumes representing the planets, among them Arcimboldo, designer of the pageant and Jacopo Strada, keeper of the Emperor's Cabinet of Curiosities.

As the convoy came close, Jan's jaw dropped. Rudolf looked nothing like he imagined an emperor would. The person before him was squat and hunched, making him appear older than his thirty-one years and, although festooned in royal insignia – imperial crown on his head, orb and sceptre in his hands – he looked world-weary. Greta couldn't take her eyes off him.

"He looks sad," said Jan.

"That's the curse of his family line. They're all afflicted with unsteady temperaments. One moment given over to emotional theatrics, the next drowning in melancholia."

Swept up by the crowd, they followed the pageant across the bridge from the Lesser Quarter, all the way to the cobbled Old Town Square, where people jostled to catch a glimpse of the manmade volcano that had been constructed at its centre. A carnival of elephants and figures from mythology circled it: Medusa with her headdress of snakes, Vlasta the Bohemian Warrior flanked by spear-bearing maidens, then a vision of monstrous beauty in the form of three winged women straddling black stallions. The crowd shrank as they unfurled their wings and the horses reared.

"What are they?" Jan gasped.

"The Furies of ancient legend," Greta explained, her eyes glowing. "The Sisters of Vengeance."

A row of men stepped forward and lit fires at the foot of the volcano before the Emperor's entourage left in a flurry of smoke and flames as five chimes rang across the Square. Jan looked up and saw a carved skeletal representation of Death emerge from a door beneath the face of the astronomical clock. He shivered.

"Fine piece of work, isn't it?"

They turned and saw a young man. He was tall and slim, his hair sleek and black, his features sharp.

"It's a shame the fellow who made it suffered such a cruel fate. He was blinded by the authorities, to prevent him from replicating the work somewhere else.

But that's the risk innovators take. People come to resent you. They envy your talent and riches," he said, flicking imaginary specks from his cape.

"Forgive me," he continued, extending a hand towards Greta. She noticed the ring on his middle finger; a band of polished bone adorned with a ram's head. "Ignaz Muller."

Greta didn't usually respond to such forthrightness, but she had to admit there was something charismatic about this man. He had such piercing eyes. She introduced herself.

"Charmed," he said. "Your feathered beauty caught my eye from across the Square. Such exquisite plumage. I've never seen such gorgeousness," he smiled, fixing his gaze on Greta.

"It was a gift from my husband, Doctor Gustav Grausam, the prominent Viennese scientist. He created it. There's not another in the whole world."

"I'm sure there's not. Grausam. Yes, I've heard the name. I've read some of his papers. I shall look forward to making his acquaintance."

"That won't be possible," Greta replied. "He died a few weeks ago. Suddenly."

"I'm sorry to hear of your loss, and I wish you well here. Where are you staying?" he asked, glancing around him. "Do you have property here? Or family?"

"We have no immediate plans. But, naturally, I have means to secure lodgings until we find permanent accommodation."

"I was his apprentice," Jan blurted out, keen to make an impression. "I'm going to study to be a doctor."

"Is that so?" replied Ignaz. "And who might you be?"

"This is Jan. My husband's nephew" said Greta. The stranger's impudence was beginning to irritate her.

"Forgive my scepticism," Ignaz replied with a graceful

bow, "I meant no offence, but you'll soon see for yourselves that this city swarms with tricksters and would-be magicians. I advise you to beware of those who claim to have transformed dung into diamonds, or turned ditch water into liquid gold. They're mostly liars and thieves. But," he continued, "I suggest we lay any misunderstanding aside. I can help you find lodgings. I know all the best hotels and besides, I won't hear of such a fine-looking lady being left to fend unaided in a strange city."

"Very well," Greta agreed, confident she was more than capable of looking after herself, but very satisfied to see her allure was as potent as ever.

"Then follow me."

As they walked, she told Ignaz about her life in Vienna, described the lavish conditions she was used to living in, and explained she would settle for nothing less than luxurious surroundings. "I trust you were speaking the truth when you said you knew the best hotels."

Only after three attempts did Ignaz find a place that met Greta's expectations. The first had been too grubby, the second located on too noisy a street. But this, the third, had been deemed satisfactory: a suite of two tastefully furnished rooms in a guest house somewhere in the north of Prague.

"Not quite what I'm accustomed too, but it will do for now. Thank you for your assistance," said Greta, setting down her bird. She opened the door to show Ignaz out.

"I appreciate you must be exhausted after your long journey this evening but, if you'll permit, I'd be honoured if you'd accompany me to a private salon of alchemy tomorrow. I think its distinguished patrons would be interested in hearing about your late husband's work. Very interested indeed."

"Do you think so?" asked Greta, her grey eyes meeting his.

"I'm not sure that's a good idea," Jan cut in. "I'm the custodian of his work now he's ... now Gustav's gone.

"I shall come for you at eight o'clock," Ignaz said to Greta, his gaze never leaving hers.

The city's fine robes fell away as Greta and Jan followed Ignaz to the House of the Hidden in Prague's Ghetto district next evening – street by street, layer by layer – until it was left shivering in a set of shabby rags. Gone were the well-kept properties Jan had seen around Old Town Square. Here the houses were made from timber or clay, some so crooked it seemed they might sink into the ground. The air changed too; the stench of stagnant water, waste matter and rotting vegetables rose from the damp alleys, and grey smoke smouldered from the roofs of tumbledown buildings.

Jan hung back behind Greta and Ignaz, still clutching his sack of books and serum. He'd never seen such filth, not in the village where he'd grown up, and certainly not in the areas of Vienna he'd got to know. He was aware they looked out of place here, ripe for being robbed, especially Greta. While she pressed her silver pomander to her nose, he pulled his overcoat close and ran to catch them, wondering how they'd find their way out of this labyrinth if Ignaz didn't escort them back.

"I realise this is no place for a lady," Ignaz acknowledged, placing his cape around Greta's shoulders and steering her down the Passage of the Wolf's Throat. It was so narrow they were forced to walk in single file.

"This is no place for anyone. Too much sickness, too many beggars, too many crooks. But that's why the House of the Hidden is here, to prevent people from stumbling upon it. Only the initiated know of its existence. Like many of the strange stories spawned by this decaying district. Take this house, for example," he said pointing to the crumbling baroque building ahead of them. "Two hundred years ago it was home to Prince Vaclav of Opava, a keen amateur alchemist. Today it's owned by one of the Emperor's astrologers, a certain Jakub Krucinek, whose youngest son murdered his eldest during a fight over the treasure the Prince had stashed here. Most unfortunate, especially given that the treasure had long since been plundered and sold. But you see what I mean; this place has many ghosts. And here we are," he announced with a dramatic wave of an arm. "I promise you won't regret crossing the threshold of the House of the Hidden."

"This place?" Greta sneered. They'd stopped outside a ramshackle wooden building. It had no windows, nor a door, as far as she could see. "Is it safe?"

Ignoring her concerns, Ignaz reached behind a panel of wood and tugged the length of rope it concealed. A bell sounded and the panel opened to reveal the shrivelled face of an old woman.

"You're back," she croaked, pulling her woollen shawl tight to her chin.

"Of course," Ignaz replied.

"It's been a while, but I knew you would be." She leaned forward and scrutinised Greta, then Jan. She reminded him of a walnut. "New company?" she sniffed. "And smart, too. That'll cost you. I can't let you off for being handsome," she said, winking.

"I understand. You have your job to do, as I have mine." Ignaz turned to Greta. "Do you have a few coins?"

"Well," she replied, flustered. "I do, but ..."

"Then give her three."

Greta did as he said and the crone grinned toothlessly. "This way," she beckoned with a curl of her crooked finger.

Once inside, Jan was struck by the babble of many different languages. German, Czech, English, Polish, Spanish, Italian and many more he couldn't recognise at all. The patrons' extravagant outfits contrasted with the sparseness of the room, which was bare but for a few benches, tables and a serving hatch. There was an edge to the atmosphere, a heady brew of energy and tension, and Jan soon understood why.

"Perhaps I should I show one of these men Gustav's elixir," Greta mused.

"No!" cried Jan. "It's too soon."

"He's right," Ignaz agreed. "You wouldn't want anyone to steal your husband's work and pass it off as their own, would you? Take my advice, bide your time until you know who you can trust."

Jan glared at Ignaz.

Greta surveyed the room. "Who are all these people?" she asked. "Do you know them?" She was aware that apart from the serving girl and crone on the door, she was the only woman in the room.

"Of course. Well, most of them. Many of Rudolf's men come here, performing feats of transformation and conjuration, acting as his eyes and ears, on the lookout for new talent to bring to the royal court. That's Oswald Croll," he gestured, "a German professor of medicine and alchemy, and Rudolf's personal physician. He prepares amulets for the royal household, and claims his formula of powdered toads and blood can ward off the plague."

"Really?" said Jan. "Do you think it can?" He longed to meet this man.

"I haven't seen proof myself, but that's not to say it isn't true." He glanced around the room. "Proceedings will begin soon. There's space over there. After you, good lady."

But Jan was too enthralled by the conversations around him to follow them to the back of the room. It seemed that most of the authors of Gustav's books were here, in this modest looking meeting place for the world's sharpest minds. While Ignaz and Greta chatted at their table, he sidled up to the group that had gathered around Michael Sendiv.

"As I'll prove in my next book, *The New Chemical Light*, our science is not a dream, as the vulgar and foolish often suppose. Rather, our science is real and seeks to reveal the truth of life. If, like myself, a person is able to transmute metal into gold or silver, he may be said to have opened the Gates of Nature. But take note of three things, my friends," he warned. "First, if you do not follow the guidance of Nature your efforts will be pointless. Secondly, mix only things which are like each other, and separate opposing elements with heat. Thirdly, the true meaning of our philosophy will be unintelligible to the arrogant, the boastful and the mocking. Beware of those who exhibit such traits."

Without thinking, Jan raised a hand above the rapt crowd and found himself questioning Sendiv's declaration.

"But don't many scientific experiments involve mixing things which aren't alike?"

The young man standing beside Sendiv sniggered. "How would you know?" he scoffed, although he couldn't have been much older than Jan himself.

Everyone turned to see who'd dared challenge the eminent chemist. Jan felt his cheeks burn. *At least it's dark*, he thought.

"Didn't you hear what I just said about those who mock?" Sendiv scolded.

He turned to Jan. "Do you have an example we might discuss?"

Jan cleared his throat and stood tall. "I suppose it all depends how you classify things, and what you mean by saying one thing is *like* or different from another. I mean ..."

Before he had a chance to explain further a gong sounded and a voice came from the serving hatch.

"Welcome Rabbi Loew, Imparter of Arcane Wisdom, Advisor to Emperor Rudolf II."

Still shaking with exhilaration, Jan positioned himself at the front of the performance area. He knew he'd been right to speak out, and he knew he hadn't appeared foolish. Far from it. He'd devoured Sendiv's writings in Gustav's library, and had understood every word. And besides, hadn't Gustav always urged him to question things?

Jan watched closely as an elderly black-robed man took to the floor. He stood completely still, eyes shut fast in concentration, arms relaxed at his sides. A towering figure of composure and authority. The guests glanced sidelong at one another, waiting for something to happen. After several minutes, something did.

Sugar-coated fruits, jugs of fine wines and platters laden with succulent meat materialised on each table. Sumptuous tapestries appeared on the mouldy walls. The intoxicating aroma of patchouli and cedarwood filled the air. Candle stumps were replaced with polished oil lamps.

Jan stared open-mouthed at the scene before him, astounded by the Rabbi's transformation of the sparsely furnished inn into a treasure trove. Was it an illusion? Or was he some kind of magician?

Loew raised a hand to silence the babble of his spectators. "Prepare to hear about a far higher act of transformation; the story of how I created a golem, a man of mud, in the manner of my forefathers."

"I remember hearing about that," whispered a man behind Jan to his companion. "Very strange business, but if there's anyone I'd believe capable of such a thing, it's Loew."

Jan edged closer, impatient to hear the wise man's tale.

The Man of Clay

*A*ccording to the old texts, the creation of a golem requires the coming together of the four elements so one morning, three years ago, I called upon my son-in-law to represent fire, my disciple to represent water, while I represented air. Fashioned from clay, the golem would represent the fourth element of earth.

We purified ourselves for three days and on the fourth day we swathed ourselves in white robes and proceeded to the Vltava River where we kneaded, rolled and shaped the dark red clay of its banks into the form of a man, my golem. We stood at its feet awhile, silently watching the lifeless lump.

Now ready to proceed, I asked my son-in-law to walk around it seven times, starting from the right hand side. It began to glow red with heat. Next I asked my disciple to do likewise, only starting from the left. A gust of steam rushed from the golem's torso. It became moist, hair began to sprout from its head, nails forced their way through the tips of its fingers.

Finally, after walking around the golem myself, I etched the word EMET on a clay tablet and placed it in its mouth, for EMET means truth and the golem's job was to be true to my wishes, to assist me in spreading the truth of my people through the city, and to protect them from danger.

Then I bowed to the east, to the west, to the north and the south and the golem opened his eyes.

"On your feet!" I ordered and the golem stood. I dressed him, named him Josef and charged him with obeying my every word. My mute giant of mud nodded. He was to work for me every day of the week except Saturday, when he would rest, malleable in character as he was in body.

Josef Golem assisted me in everything I did, and every Friday at sunset I would rub out the first letter inscribed on the tablet, leaving only the word MET, which means Death, so he could rest. But one Friday, preoccupied with my daughter's illness, I forgot to remove the letter and while I was at work the golem ran amok, bored and unable to function without my instructions.

From inside the synagogue I heard cries of "Josef Golem has gone crazy!" I rushed outside and saw his bloated body rampaging through the streets, destroying all that obstructed him. His swollen hands tore heads from chickens. His thick legs trampled down market stalls. I ran towards him, rubbed the first letter from his mouth and called out, "Go home and lie down!" And my blood-and-feather-smeared servant became as meek as a lamb and lumbered home behind me. I suppose I was lucky. Golems have been known to turn on their creators.

The time came for my work with Josef to end so my son-in-law, disciple and I went to his bed one night and did exactly as we had done when we created him, only in reverse. I undressed him, then bowed to the south, to the north, to the west and finally to the east. I rubbed out the first letter etched into the tablet, leaving only the word MET, which means Death. I walked around him seven times. His hair and nails retreated, his body became dry. My disciple walked around him seven times from the right. My son-in-law walked around him seven times from the left. We stood at his head awhile, watching him return to his original lifeless form.

And that, gentlemen, is how I created and destroyed the golem – Josef Golem – a man made from the earth, who returned to the earth whence he came.

Jan wondered if Gustav had known that while they were in Vienna perfecting their serum and beginning to fashion a mandrake man, here in Prague someone had made a man from mud. He caught Loew's eye. The Rabbi went to him, laid a hand on his shoulder.

"I know you," he said, his voice deep and resonant.

"I ... I don't think so," Jan replied. "I'm not from here. We only arrived yesterday."

"I can see in your eyes that you've been touched by Death's monstrous hand. I'm sorry for your loss. Be thankful you've been spared." Then the Rabbi left.

Jan rushed to tell Greta about his encounter, but her table was empty. He looked around the room but she and Ignaz were nowhere to be seen. The only trace of them having been there was a single peacock feather next to Greta's chair.

"Excuse me," he asked the serving girl. "There were two people here. A lady with a birdcage and a man. Did you see where they went?"

"It's not my place to watch what the guests get up to. Everyone's business is their own here."

Jan rushed outside. No sign of anyone. He sprinted up the passageway and called again. Nothing but a stray dog. He turned onto the next street, then the next, his teeth chattering, his heart pounding so hard he could feel it in his ears. The stench of dirt and disease seemed even stronger. He now felt certain they should never have trusted Ignaz. What if he'd made off with Greta? What if she was in real danger?

Jan couldn't take any more and, as the toll of death knells began to ring through the Ghetto, he fell to the floor, exhausted. He felt a lump beneath him but couldn't find the energy to move. Not even when he noticed that the lump was a dead rat, frozen into a puddle. Not even when he saw a figure emerge from the shadows and come towards him.

Not even when he felt the figure standing directly over him. He was too weak, too tired, even to cry.

Chapter Nine
Angel of the Ghetto

The figure had been watching Jan since he'd fled the House of the Hidden. It had seen him dash from one dead end to the next, initially suspicious he'd done something wrong and was desperate to escape the scene of a crime. Why else would he have been in such a panic? Then the figure heard his sobs, and it became clear that something was wrong.

"Hello? Can you hear me?"

Jan opened his eyes.

It was a girl. A strikingly beautiful girl, wrapped in a long white fur coat and haloed by moonlight. She seemed about the same age as Jan, and they had similarly slim builds, but that was where their physical likeness ended. In every other respect she was Jan's opposite. Where his hair was wavy and fair, hers was sleek and black. Where Jan's face was freckled and brown from long summers spent outdoors, hers was porcelain white, as if it had never been exposed to the sun. And their eyes too. Jan's were deep indigo, while the girl's irises were like pale thin bands of moonstone.

"Are you sick?" she asked, leaning over him. Her voice was warm, her words clearly enunciated.

"I have to find her. My Aunt Greta."

"I'll help you look, if you like," the girl said. "It's easy to get lost here." She noticed Jan was shaking, that his face was blotched with tear stains. "Don't worry, she can't have gone far. Where are you staying? She's probably waiting for you there."

"That's just it. I have no idea. A man we met at the Emperor's parade brought us to a guest house last night. We rested there all day, and he took us to the alchemists' inn along that alley this evening. It was dark, and I wasn't paying attention."

Jan held his head in his hands as he tried to visualise the guest house. He remembered the row of trees outside, that the buildings were stout, that there'd been a dog chained outside the first house on the road. But that was all. He didn't know the name of the guest house, nor the name of the street, nor even the name of the district.

"It's no good," he said, shaking his head in despair. "All I know is that one moment Greta was in the inn and the next she'd gone. What am I going to do?"

"Let's check the area before the night frost sets in," said the girl, brushing a strand of hair from her face. "She can't have gone far."

"But what about your family? Won't they wonder where you are?"

"Don't worry about me. Tell me, why are you here? What about your parents?"

As they scoured the streets for Greta – first the warren of passages near the House of the Hidden, then a wide radius around Old Town Square – Jan told the girl how he and Greta had come to be in Prague. He was hesitant at first, reluctant to reveal too much, given that he suspected Ignaz – like her, a stranger – was responsible for Greta's disappearance but as they walked on, Jan was soothed by her company.

"It makes my worries seem like nothing," she sighed. "You should shelter in one of these arcades for the night, out of the wind. You're exhausted, and we've done all we can tonight. We'll find her tomorrow."

Jan shook his head. "I can't rest. I remember the way back to the House of the Hidden. I'll wait for her there. She's bound to go back to look for me."

"No, you mustn't go back to the Ghetto alone," the girl told him. "It's not safe to linger there long. The air's bad. It's a breeding ground for the plague. And it can be more dangerous at night."

"So why were you there?" Jan asked.

"I'll come back in the morning," she said, sidestepping his question. "We can search together. Now promise me you'll rest tonight."

"I will." As worried as he was about Greta, as much as he wanted to keep searching, Jan knew he had little choice. He was overcome with exhaustion. "I'm Jan, by the way. Who are you?"

"The Angel of the Ghetto," she smiled. "That's who I am."

"I mean what's your name?"

She paused. "I'm Zuzana. You can call me Zuzana."

Chapter Ten
At the Place of the Black Bear

Next morning, Jan was woken by the chimes of the astronomical clock striking six. He sat bolt upright, paralysed with panic as he realised he wasn't at home in his bed in the House of the Seven Stars. He wasn't even in Vienna. It all came back to him: he'd spent the night on the streets in a strange city and Greta had gone. Somehow, he couldn't shake the feeling that Ignaz was to blame.

Why? he thought. *Why would he have taken her? Because she was rich? Because he thought she might have access to the serum?* But Jan knew he had no proof of this, that anything might have happened. Ignaz himself had warned of the dangers of the Ghetto, and Greta's attire would have made her an obvious target for thieves. Zuzana had said it wasn't safe there at night too. Zuzana! He hoped he *would* see her again.

"Out of my way!" bawled a tradesman on his way to Old Town Square.

"Sorry," said Jan, hastening to move. But, as the man's barrow bashed into his ankle, he felt his anger rise. He took a deep breath and tried to think logically, as Gustav would have done.

His first thought was for Greta's safety. His second was for his work. He had to keep his promise to Gustav. His third was how he would survive if he didn't find Greta soon. He had nothing but his sack and the clothes on his back.

Jan decided to find his way back to the House of the Hidden, in case there was any sign of Greta there. As he neared the Passage of the Wolf's Throat bright sunlight streamed down. By day the Ghetto seemed less sinister but, without the mantle of night to obscure it, the poverty of the place and its people seemed starker still. He'd begun to piece together the geography of the district. There was one main street, with several smaller avenues leading from it, and from them stemmed the tiny passageways he'd lost himself in the previous night. All this was confined within four gates that served both to protect the inhabitants from attack, and to ensure they lived according to the law.

For a while he watched pedlars selling cloth and candles from carts and trays hung around their necks, old women trading poppy bread from their windows for logs and milk. He passed butchers, tailors, cobblers and glassmakers, and the Perlsticker textile workshop whose tapestries were famed throughout Europe, according to the sign above the door.

Jan continued to the Great Synagogue and the Town Hall next door, then went west to the Old Jewish Cemetery. He peered through the gates at the graves. Had he been able to understand their script, he would have read elegies describing what the dead had done with their lives and how they'd met their death.

THE
PASSAGE
of the
WOLF'S throat

Jan saw a large congregation of mourners approaching and, from its size, assumed this was the funeral of an especially respected dweller of the district, perhaps a rabbi. But then he noticed there was more than one coffin. He counted at least a dozen, some so small that the bodies they bore must have belonged to babies and young children. *Another place of the plague ogre*, Jan thought, reminded of his own village.

Jan saw sickness mingled with sorrow in the eyes and faces of many of the mourners. *How many of their fates were already sealed? How would it feel to live as the walking dead?* A small girl caught his eye. Jan's heart clenched when she shook back her mane of ringlets and he saw the swellings on her neck. There were four of them, each the size of a hen's egg, each covered in red spots. She couldn't have been more than six. Jan knew she wouldn't live much longer. The black and blue blotches on her face indicated bleeding beneath the skin, the sign of a blood infection that her little heart was pumping around her already weakened body. The same marks had heralded the final stages of his parents' illness. After that had come the delirious fever. Then death. Jan wanted to go to her, to reach out and do something, anything, to help. But the solemn procession had entered the burial ground, such a contrast to the Emperor's decadent display.

Jan strode to the House of the Hidden, still seething with rage. The inn looked as shut and unoccupied as it had done last night, but Jan remembered Ignaz had rung a hidden bell. He felt around for it, but found nothing. The cord had gone.

"You came!" called Jan.

He'd spent the past few hours sitting near Old Town Square, shivering in the cold, at a loss as to what to do next. So to see Zuzana approaching immediately lifted his spirits.

And though her face was obscured by the hood of her cloak, Jan couldn't help but notice how much more striking she was by daylight; strong features, luminous eyes, jet-black hair offsetting her pale complexion and white stole.

"Of course. I said I would, didn't I?" she replied, crouching next to him, not giving a second thought to the fact that her skirts were trailing in the dirt and slush.

"Here, I brought you food."

As she passed him the parcel, Jan noticed a large yellow bruise on her wrist.

"How did you do that?"

"It's nothing. My eldest brother likes to play fight." She pulled down her sleeve. "Eat. You must be hungry. I hope you managed to get some rest. I didn't sleep much myself. I couldn't stop thinking about you out here. I'm so sorry I couldn't find you somewhere proper to stay, but it was already so late ..."

"Don't apologise," Jan interrupted, wondering why she was being so kind to him. "I slept well enough and went back to the Ghetto this morning, to see if there was any sign of Greta at the inn. But it was as if it had never existed. Even the hidden bell had gone."

"Of course. The House of the Hidden only exists at night."

"How do you know? The man who brought us there said it was a private place, known only to alchemists."

"I'm the Angel of the Ghetto. I know all its secrets."

Jan felt the tingle of goose bumps along his arms. "What do you mean?" he asked.

Zuzana chewed her lower lip for a moment. "If I tell you something, will you promise to keep it to yourself? I mean *really* promise?"

"Of course," Jan replied, flattered she wanted to confide in him. "You can trust me. After all you've done for me, the least I can do is keep a secret."

"I've never told *anyone* else this," she said, "but whenever I can, I come to the Ghetto. I bring food for the poor, medicine for the sick. When you said what had happened to your parents, that you want to become a doctor, I thought you might be interested in what I do. Do you know what the fastest growing occupations are here? Death cart labourers and plague pit diggers. Can you believe it? There are almost more bodies than there are people to bury them."

"I saw that this morning. I don't understand why the Emperor doesn't send his doctors to help. Why doesn't he order them to find a cure? That would be more useful than making them transform powders into gold. Doesn't it make you angry?"

"Sometimes," she replied, the light momentarily fading from her eyes. "But he has his own demons to deal with. He's sick, and has still done more for the Ghetto than his father ever did. But tell me, why were you at the House of the Hidden?"

Jan ran his fingers through his hair. Last night, as he and Zuzana had searched the Ghetto, he'd deliberately withheld specific details of his work. Gustav had warned him of strangers who'd do anything to steal scientific knowledge. And then Ignaz had said the same thing only last night. But since spending even a little time with Zuzana, he felt different. Here was a girl who had shared her own secrets, who shared his ambitions and had gone out of her way for him. So Jan told her all about the butterflies whose poison he'd been trying to render harmless, the elixir that could sustain and regenerate life. And he revealed his hope that it might one day be adapted to cure the plague.

"It's not ready yet, but soon. Then I'll have to find a way

to spread word of the serum's life-saving properties, develop it into an easily produced, readily available remedy. Everyone should have access to medicine. I'll march into the castle and tell the Emperor myself if I have to." Jan paused to catch his breath. "Although while I'm living on the streets and have no money, there's no way I can do that."

"I've already thought of that," said Zuzana. "Follow me."

It was now after noon and, while the sun still shone brightly, it was doing little to thaw the frozen city. They walked around Old Town Square to avoid the crowds and turned onto an alley nestled between the Church of St James and the Church of Our Lady Before Tyn. Jan was amazed he hadn't noticed them yesterday – it made him realise just how excessive the Emperor's display must have been if it had dwarfed these magnificent buildings. But today the twin spires of Tyn Church were reinstated as graceful guardians of the Square, visible from the furthest reaches of the city.

"You have to see this," said Zuzana, leading Jan to St James's Church. She pointed to what looked like a piece of dried meat nailed to the door. "It's a warning for thieves, if ever there was one. It's the shrunken arm of a robber who tried to steal the church's treasure over a hundred years ago. It's said a statue grabbed hold of him as he tried to leave and his arm had to be cut off to free him. Come." She took Jan's hand and led him into Tyn Courtyard.

Jan shuddered, but not because of the cold, or the gruesome spectacle of the shrivelled limb. It was because of the gentleness of Zuzana's touch. He hadn't felt this close to anyone for a long time.

"Every trader and burgher must pass through here to pay

tax on their goods before entering the city," Zuzana explained. "It's always lively, especially in the evening when merchants' guilds from all over the world gather here. They call it the Courtyard of Joy. This building, Stradovych House, belongs to the Italian side of my family."

"You're Italian?" Jan asked. "You don't sound it."

"I'm not. My family are from all over. My father's ancestors are Spanish, my mother's are from northern Italy. We've travelled a lot."

"Is this where I'm going to stay? With your relatives?"

"No, you'll stay here," she said going to the tall house next door. "The Place of the Black Bear. It's one of my father's properties. An old apothecary lived here until he died a few months ago. It couldn't be more perfect for you." She smiled. "I must have been fated to find you."

"Are you sure this is all right?" Jan asked. "I mean, won't your father mind a stranger staying in his property? I can't pay." His heart sank. "He doesn't know, does he?"

"Not exactly, but it's fine, I promise. If we're careful. Welcome to your new home."

Once inside, all Jan's reservations vanished. Although most of the rooms across the house's four storeys were unfurnished and those that did have furniture needed a good clean, there was a fire and plenty of wood to burn, a comfortable sleeping area upstairs and, best of all, the apothecary's equipment was still here, laid out on the ground floor. Glass jars and pipes for distilling. Pestle and mortars for grinding. Crucibles for heating. And jar after jar of botanical solutions and herbs.

"Even verbena," Jan noticed. "If only I still had my mandrake root."

"Mandrake?"

"Yes." Jan nodded. "We were hoping to create a living being from one, like the ancient alchemists did."

"What happened to it?"

"I don't know. It just wasn't there when I went to uproot it. I still have the elixir, though, and that's what matters. I'll never let it out of my sight."

Jan surveyed the room. "You're right. This is perfect. It has everything I need. I can start right away, although I should go back to the bridge first, before dusk falls, in case Greta returned to where our driver left us."

"Let's go together. It's on my way home, and I need to get back," Zuzana replied, twirling a strand of hair around a finger. She looked uneasy. "I've been away too long."

"I'm sorry. I didn't mean to keep you, or get you into trouble. Why don't you just tell your mother and father why you come to the Ghetto? Why do you hide it from them?

Surely they'd be proud of what you're doing. I know mine would have been. And besides, they must wonder where you are."

"They don't notice anything about me, which is just as well, I suppose. They're very strict. I'm not supposed to go out alone under any circumstances. Where or why wouldn't make any difference."

Jan wondered what kind of parents wouldn't notice their daughter was missing. But then, he knew not everyone was blessed with a family like his had been.

"Don't worry about me," Zuzana said. She'd seen Jan's face fall sad again. "And don't worry about Greta. We'll keep looking." She reached into a pocket and produced a handful of coins. "Take these. You can't be without money. And there's enough bread and meat here to last a few days. Fruit too," she said leaving her basket on the table. "Here's the key. Come and go as you please, of course, but try not to let too many people see you. I'd rather no one else knew."

"Of course. I'll be careful. And thank you for the coins. I'll repay you as soon as I can."

Jan and Zuzana found themselves caught in a fresh flurry of snowfall as they crossed Charles Bridge. While the late afternoon light was fading fast, their immediate world was white and bright as they whirled around in the sudden cascade. Zuzana led Jan to the south-facing wall of the bridge and together they watched the last rafts of the day transport loads of timber and flour into the city from the outlying villages. She pointed out the green mass of Petrin Hill, the palatial residences of the Emperor's governors and administrators, the mill workers, and fishermen mooring their boats.

"I'm going back to the House of the Hidden later," Jan said. "Won't you come with me?"

"I can't. Not this evening. Besides, I'd never go inside that place."

"Why not? Because you're a girl?" asked Jan.

"It's not that. I never let *that* stop me doing what I want," she insisted. "I just can't go there. See you tomorrow."

Jan watched her willowy frame glide beneath the Lesser Quarter gateway then climb the steep hill to the Castle District. She was rushing but looked as graceful as ever. *Like a bird of paradise,* he thought, scarcely able to believe he'd met her.

He walked down the stone steps to the riverbank, followed the course of the Brook of the Little Devil past the giant wooden wheel of the mill and tried to remember where exactly Ludwig had parked the carriage. There it was; The Three Ostriches. But there was no carriage. No Ludwig. No Greta. Jan rubbed his eyes, took a deep breath and wound his way through the Lesser Quarter. He bought himself a bowl of soup in the House of the Maltese Knights on the Lesser Town Square, bolted it down and mopped up every last drop with a crust of bread. It had been his first warm meal for days.

Nearly there, Zuzana panted as she ascended the steepest point of the hill before reaching the expansive plateau of Castle Square, but she couldn't relax until she was back in her room, ready to be called for supper, as if she'd been there all afternoon, reading or embroidering while her brothers had their lessons, or went out hunting elks and aurochs in Stromovka Park.

"You'd think someone might have noticed I've been stitching that same stupid piece of cloth for months," she muttered, quickening her step. She was angry and sad she'd had to leave Jan, but she couldn't afford to be caught, now more than ever. He needed her too, like the sick in the Ghetto needed her, and she'd be no use to anyone if she were caught. She knew she'd be locked in her room as punishment, at the very least. She hoped Jan understood. She'd never met anyone quite like him. Clever, but kind and humble too. And she'd never met anyone with such deep, dark eyes. Who would have known that the trembling figure she'd seen hunched on the ground near the Passage of the Wolf's Throat possessed such precious knowledge? She'd assumed he was a vagrant, or perhaps a servant abandoned to the streets by his master. No one could have guessed, but she knew she ought not judge by appearances. Zuzana tried to imagine how it would feel to have lost everyone as he had. She felt ashamed for having grumbled about her family, however distant they felt from her.

The light dipped beneath the peak of Petrin Hill. Zuzana pulled her hood close and hurried across Castle Square thinking how nice it would be to have someone to share her thoughts with. She knew she'd be married off to a rich nobleman one day, probably someone much older, possibly someone from a far-flung land where she'd be forced to make her home. But, for now, she intended to forestall her fate for as long as possible. She wanted to enjoy the freedom she'd created for herself, and put it to good use. She just wished she could tell Jan more about her life. He'd shared everything with her. *In time,* she thought. *Maybe soon, even.* She hoped to help him realise his ambition of using his serum to save as many lives as possible. She was bursting to tell someone about him, although she knew she couldn't. To do so would reveal her disobedience, and besides that she wasn't sure who she would tell anyway. *There's no one who cares enough.*

Zuzana slipped through a secret side gate to her father's garden. *It's as if I'm invisible. Safely unseen!*

Or so she thought.

After a meal drawn out by formalities and conversation that bored her, Zuzana went to her room. She sank into her duck down mattress and stared up at the canopy covering her bed.

Better to be alone than ignored in company, she decided. She was tired of being left out of family discussions over dinner. All anyone seemed to care about was her brothers' progress at school and success at the hunt.

One day, they'll know who I really am, what I really do.

A knock came at the door. "May I come in? May I fetch you anything?"

Zuzana sighed. It was her family's longest serving maid. "I'm fine, thank you. Just resting."

But the old woman bustled into the room regardless. She knew when something was troubling her Zuzana. "How about an extra pillow, my sweet? A tincture to settle your nerves? You seemed distracted all through dinner. What's on your mind?"

Zuzana sat up and clutched her knees to her chin. "May I ask you something?"

"Of course," said the maid, stroking Zuzana's hair. "But don't crinkle your nose so. You'll give yourself wrinkles. That's better. Now, you may ask me whatever you like. I don't claim to be learned, but I've lived long enough in this world to enjoy the wisdom that experience brings."

"Do you believe people can change their fate, or do you think our lives are mapped out before us? I mean, do you think we're each doomed to die a certain death?"

"You shouldn't be filled with such morbid thoughts. You

should be thinking of your future husband. You'll be found a fine match, I'm sure. You need never worry about anything."

Zuzana frowned. "That's what I mean. Why *must* my life be laid out like that? What about what I want? But, more than that, I was thinking of the sick, those suffering with the plague. Surely you don't believe they were born to live such lives? That they were born to die such painful deaths? *I* don't believe that's true."

"Don't ask me to explain the whys and wherefores, but if there's one thing I've learned in this world, it's that there's no escaping fate. I'm not saying they deserve it, only that things happen for reasons beyond our control."

"Lady Fortune knows what she wants for each of us, and there's no way round that. She spins our fates, plots the course of our lives as she rides her Wheel of Life, and woe betide anyone who dares try to defy her. Nothing but trouble comes from meddling with the natural order of things. Let me tell you the tale of a foolish girl who tried to do just that."

Rusalka the Spinner and the Devil Boy of Straw

*L*ong ago, in a small village in southern Moravia, a group of girls would gather each week for a spinning party where they gossiped and giggled and shared secrets while turning coarse wool into fine thread. And every week all the girls would boast that this boy or that boy was keen on them, or reveal they were keen on this boy or that boy. All, that is, except quiet Rusalka who sat and spun in silence, even while the other girls teased her.

"When will you find yourself a boy to like you?" they mocked week after week. "Why don't you make yourself a pretend boy if you can't find a real one?" Then, one bitterly cold night, the idea came to them; they would make Rusalka a boy from straw! The biggest girl took a ladder, climbed to the roof of the house and pulled a sheaf from the roof. Then the group fashioned it into the form of a boy, dressed him in a smock and sat him next to Rusalka.

"Sweet Rusalka, meet your love!" the girls laughed. "Why don't you go to the dance with him, for this boy of straw is the only boy you're destined to have."

Rusalka's cheeks burned bright red and, with a flutter of her skirts and toss of her hair, she left the gathering, taking the straw boy with her, crying "I'll show you my destiny! May the devil come and make this boy real!"

Rusalka ran home and went straight to her room. She placed the boy of straw on a chair in the corner of the room and sobbed herself to sleep.

Later that night, Rusalka heard a match strike. She looked up and saw a handsome young man, as alive as you or I, sitting where she'd left the boy of straw. Rusalka rubbed her eyes, unable to believe what she'd seen. But, when she looked again, there was no young man, and no boy of straw. Just an empty chair.

Next week, Rusalka went as usual to the spinning party, for she loved to spin and was determined not to let the nasty girls spoil everything for her.

"Where's your boyfriend?" they laughed when she took her usual place at the back of the room. "Has even he deserted you?"

But Rusalka held her head high and told them how her boy of straw had transformed into a handsome young man. Then, as they all screeched with laughter, the same handsome young man appeared in the room and sat beside Rusalka. He behaved like a true gentleman all night, passing the girls new thread when they needed it, lighting new candles when the stumps of the old burned out, offering them succulent meat snacks when they felt hungry. But it was clear to all that he only had eyes for Rusalka. He tended to her every need as if she were a princess, and he her devoted suitor. At the end of the evening he escorted Rusalka home, leaving the other girls wondering how a boy of straw could be transformed into a living being.

The same thing happened the next week, and the next and the next, and Rusalka never felt so happy as when the handsome young man was at her side. But, every week after escorting her home, he would vanish into the depths of the night and only reappear at the next gathering. This saddened Rusalka greatly, for she had no idea where or why he went, so she sought advice from a wise old woman.

"Innocent Rusalka," said the wise old woman. "The answer is simple. When he next appears, attach a length of fine thread to his clothing and keep hold of the other end. Then, when he leaves, you can follow the thread to find him."

So, the next time the young man appeared, Rusalka did just that. As he leaned to light a fresh candle, she took a length of fine thread and attached it to the bottom of his trousers with a single stitch. After he'd escorted her home and vanished into the night Rusalka followed the trail of the thread. It led her through the village, through the woods, into the churchyard, and right up to the ossuary, final resting place of hundreds of human skeletons.

Rusalka peeped inside and let out a gasp of horror, for within the walls of this house of bones was her handsome young man, dancing among the dead like a demented devil. Aghast, she saw him pick through the skeletons with a grotesque grin on his face and a wild stare in his eyes. Whenever he found a piece of flesh left on a bone, he would gnaw it with relish, as it if were one of the meaty snacks he'd offered the girls at their gatherings. And whenever he found a piece of fat he would fashion it into a candle that looked just like the ones he'd brought to the spinning parties.

Rusalka ran home as fast as her legs would carry her, vowing never to go to another spinning party, in case this boy of straw who had turned into a handsome young man who had turned out to be a devil, appeared to her there again. But, that very same night, as the clock struck twelve, she heard a tapping at her window. It was him.

"Rusalka, Rusalka, meek as can be,
What did you see when you followed me?"

"I saw nothing," said Rusalka, for she knew that to tell him would mean surrendering her soul to him forevermore.

"You lie," he replied,
"I can see in your eyes.
And so on this night your brother shall die!"

Sadly, these words came true and at dawn Rusalka learned that her brother had passed away. Directly after his funeral, the man appeared to Rusalka again, singing,

"Rusalka, Rusalka, meek as can be,
What did you see when you followed me?"

"I saw nothing," Rusalka repeated.

"You lie," he replied,
"I can see in your eyes.
And so on this night your sister shall die!"

Once again, these words came true and Rusalka's sister died and after her so too did Rusalka's mother and father until there was no one left but Rusalka herself. Fearing she would be next, Rusalka her went to her neighbours and told them what to do when her time came.

"Instead of carrying my coffin through the cottage door, you must dig a hole beneath the threshold and remove it through that since according to custom if a body is at risk of possession by bad spirits, as mine surely will be, it must be removed in this way to protect its passage to the next world. Then, once outside, you must attach the coffin to a horse and bury me whenever it stops."

That night the man appeared to her again, singing,

"Rusalka, Rusalka, meek as can be,
What did you see when you followed me?"
"I saw nothing," said Rusalka.

"You lie," he replied,
"I can see in your eyes.
And so on this night you too shall die!"

That night, Rusalka passed away and so her neighbours
dug a hole beneath the threshold. But it wasn't quite big
enough so they ended up carrying her coffin through the
door. Then they attached it to a horse and buried her where
the horse stopped, which was at a crossroads where three
roads met.

Some months later, when spring came, Rusalka grew from
her grave in the form of a brilliant white flower. A
gentleman passing the flower ordered his servant boy to step
down from the carriage and pick it for him, for he'd never
seen such a beautiful blossom. But when the servant went to
pluck it from the earth, it vanished before his eyes, as if he'd
been blinded by its beauty.

"I see no flower, Master," said the boy, scratching his
head. "It's gone."

"Foolish boy!" shouted the gentleman, for he could see the
blooming beauty as clearly as he could see his own hands.
"Driver, step down and pick it for me."

So the gentleman's driver went to pick the flower and the
same thing happened. It vanished before his eyes, as if he'd
been blinded by its beauty.

"There's no flower," he said, shaking his head. "The boy was right."

Now beside himself with anger, the gentleman stepped down from the carriage himself and pulled the blossom from the earth. "See!" he exclaimed, placing it in his hat for safe keeping.

That night, after dining on an enormous feast, the gentleman sat his hat on the dressing table and went to bed. As soon as he fell asleep, the pure white flower in his hat transformed into a beautiful young woman. It was Rusalka! She felt desperately hungry but after searching the whole house for something to eat, she found not a morsel.

"I have thirst and I have hunger
Yet he consumed it all before his slumber,"

she sang sadly before returning to the form of a flower.

Next morning, the gentleman woke to find his house in disarray. He asked his servant boy if he'd noticed anything unusual, but the boy had neither heard nor seen a thing so the gentleman ordered him to hide in an alcove and look out for anything unusual.

That night, as he kept watch from his hiding place, the boy witnessed the flower transform into beautiful Rusalka. Once again, she searched all the cupboards and cabinets for something to eat. At last she found a crust of bread.

"I have thirst and I have hunger
At least he left me some before his slumber,"

she sang before going to the gentleman and kissing his cheek three times to thank him. Moments later, Rusalka returned to the form of a flower. Next morning, the boy told his master all he'd seen and his master became consumed by a desire to meet the beautiful maiden. So, before he went to bed that night, the gentleman ordered his cook to prepare a feast. Then he lay in bed, pretending to be asleep. As the clock struck twelve the gentleman saw the hat tremble and the beautiful flower transform into an even more beautiful maiden. When she saw the feast laid out on the table, Rusalka's eyes sparkled with delight. Then she went to the gentleman and kissed him three times. But, as she turned to leave the man grabbed her and wouldn't let go so Rusalka turned herself into a toad, then a snake and then a lizard, but no matter what form she took, she couldn't escape his clutches.

But the man meant Rusalka no harm. "I'll release you if you agree to marry me and return to the form of a beautiful maiden. I'll treat you well and feed you well and give you a good life," he promised.

So Rusalka agreed to marry the gentleman and it came to pass that they were married and had a beautiful baby daughter they named Rusalka, for the child looked exactly like her mother.

After some years Rusalka was persuaded to return to the churchyard for a village festival, but the moment she found herself alone, the boy of straw who'd transformed into a handsome young man appeared at her side, saying,

"I've searched for you high, I've searched for you low
You shall be mine when the moon is aglow."

That night the young man appeared outside her room, exactly as he'd done so many years before. Rusalka shuddered as she heard his voice whisper through the window.

"Rusalka, Rusalka, meek as can be,
What did you see when you followed me?
Do not fib and do not lie
Speak the truth or your child shall die."

This time Rusalka told him everything she'd seen him do in the house of bones, that she'd spied him gnawing flesh from human skeletons and creating candles from human fat. As soon as she'd finished speaking her body and soul were surrendered to him forever and she was buried again at the crossroads and from her grave sprouted a single white flower that blossomed all year round. To this day, whenever people pass by they say, "There lies Rusalka, who did as best she could for as long as she could, until Fate tracked her down and delivered her to her Devil."

"Get some rest, now, my sweet," said the maid, kissing Zuzana's forehead. "You must be alert for your embroidery lesson in the morning."

Zuzana knew her maid meant well, but what did she care about a stupid embroidery lesson? And what did she care for a stupid husband? And she definitely didn't agree that fate should be left well alone.

Surely it's our duty to understand what makes the wheel spin, to try to change its course, to make peoples' lives better? That's why I visit the Ghetto. That's why Jan works on his serum.

There has to be hope. Even through the darkest days, like the flower that burst forth from Rusalka's grave, there must be hope that things can change.

Chapter Eleven
The Mirror of Opposites

"Yes?" said the doorkeeper, peering through the hatch in the door. Jan could just about see her sharp nose and bloodshot eyes. "So the runaway returns," she croaked. "Alone this evening?"

"Yes." He nodded. "I'm alone. My aunt went missing last night. I don't suppose you've seen her? Or the man who brought us here? Does he come often?"

"Ignaz Muller? Some weeks he's here every night. Other times I don't see him for months. But no, he hasn't been in tonight. I imagine he and your aunt are entertaining themselves in other ways," she cackled. "He's always been partial to the company of fine-looking women. Especially ones with money."

"It's not funny." Jan glared. "She might be in danger."

"If you tell me where you live, I'll send word when he comes back. For a small price, of course," she said, opening the door and cupping a hand beneath Jan's nose.

"I'm not really staying anywhere," he said after a while,

unable to bring himself to betray the promise he'd made to
Zuzana. Besides, he wasn't sure he could trust this woman.
"I'll keep looking myself. May I come in? In case they come
later."

"For a small price."

Jan reached into his pocket and passed her one of the coins
Zuzana had given him.

The House of the Hidden was just as busy that evening,
crowded with alchemists and scientists and their ambitious
young apprentices. Jan slipped between the chattering
groups, keeping an eye out for Ignaz and Greta. He ordered
a small tankard of ale and helped himself to the fruits laid out
on the tables, wondering if this was the same food Rabbi
Loew had magicked last night. He recognised a few faces, like
Oswald Croll and Michael Sendiv deep in conversation. And
there were other illustrious guests too: Arcimboldo the artist
and Tycho Brahe, the maverick Danish astrologer who'd
predicted the coming of the comets and foretold that Rudolf
would share the same fate as his lion. Jan couldn't work out
why, but there was something strange about this elaborately-
moustached man. He couldn't stop staring. Then he realised;
his nose was silver.

Jan felt a tug on his sleeve. He looked down and saw a man
dressed in a red and green jester's costume. He barely reached
Jan's waist.

"If you don't stop gawking at my master, you might find
your snout sliced off by a sword too."

"Sorry. I didn't mean ... Sorry."

"I'm only teasing, lad, but you want to be careful here. This lot may be educated gentlemen, for the most part, but they wouldn't think twice about pulling a sword on anyone who crossed them."

Jan glanced around the room, not sure how he'd ever know who to trust here.

"It's the same inside the castle too," the man added, puffing out his chest. "It's not enough to have a sharp mind; to survive in the world of alchemy you need a sharp sword too, and eyes in the back of your head."

"Have you been to the castle?" asked Jan, edging closer.

"Of course," he scoffed. "My master, Tycho Brahe, the man you were staring at, is the Emperor's personal astrologer. I live with his family in a palace to the north of Prague but, when here, we always stay in the castle. Tycho observes the skies from the Belvedere Palace in the Royal Gardens."

"What's he like?" asked Jan, scarcely able to believe he was in the company of a member of Rudolf's court for the second time in as many days.

"The Emperor? He seems to spend most of his time in his Chamber of Curiosities so I've hardly seen him. Perhaps it's just as well, seeing as he's prone to such terrible rages of madness. Probably better he locks himself away with his strange objects."

"What kinds of objects? Have you seen inside the Chambers?"

"Ancient artefacts, roots that look like little men, mechanical furniture. That kind of thing. But, I cannot lie. I've never seen for myself, and I doubt I ever shall. Few people are invited into those hallowed halls. Anyway, my Master's beckoning. I didn't even ask what brings you to this place, but perhaps our paths will cross again."

Jan hoped their paths would cross again, for that might present him with further opportunity to talk to Tycho and his associates. He was eager for such men to consider him part of their world of wisdom and discovery. He didn't want to remain an outsider for long.

But, as Jan watched the revered astrologer vacate the room with a theatrical sweep of his deep-blue cloak he suddenly felt very out of place. After a night on the streets and a day spent searching them, his clothes were crumpled, his boots splattered with mud. He decided to leave.

The Place of the Black Bear was bitterly cold. Jan could see his breath before him even after he'd closed the door behind him. Its low curved ceilings and walls were bare stone, and there were no rugs or curtains. But at least he had somewhere to stay. He sank into an armchair, closed his eyes and released a long, deep breath. He didn't dare think what might have become of him if he hadn't met Zuzana. Not only did he have a roof over his head, but he had his own laboratory, however basic it was, and however temporary his time at the Place of the Black Bear might turn out to be. But, already, he'd come to expect the unexpected in this city of surprises. Exhausted, Jan unpacked his bag, shelved the books, lined up the bottles of serum on the table. "First thing tomorrow," he said.

Jan went to the bedroom at the top of the house, four floors up, and fell into bed. As he drifted off, his mind meandered through the astonishing experiences he'd already had in Prague. It was as if the whole city was one big house of the hidden, a place of secrets and contradictions. A place where the greatest wonders lay beyond the grimiest walls, and where a broken leader slumped behind the facade of imperial pomp. Here the poor of the Ghetto lived alongside the wealthy merchants of Tyn Courtyard. Here mud could be made into men, and noses could be silver.

Jan could make no sense of it. Moments after Greta had

disappeared, a stranger had appeared from the mists to help him, while keeping her life secret from those closest to her.

"Everything's the opposite of itself here," he murmured, drifting into sleep.

Chapter Twelve
The House of the Family of Phantoms

Next morning Jan went directly down to the apothecary's den. He unpacked Gustav's robes and held them to his face. In an instant, their scent transported him back to their first hours together in the laboratory of the House of the Seven Stars. He dressed himself in them with ceremony, thinking of that momentous morning, when it seemed a happier period was about to dawn.

After laying out all the equipment he needed to retest the elixir, Jan walked to the well outside the Place of the Black Bear and drew a pail of water. He splashed his face, shook the drips from his hair and noticed that the sky was a brilliant blue and the snow had all but melted away. The sun burned bright through the cherry blossom trees: another new cycle of life had begun. He thought of the look of joy in Gustav's eyes when he'd shown him his most recent sample of serum and reasoned that since his uncle had never been wrong about anything, it really must be close to perfection.

After spending a few hours grinding, distilling, heating and blending, the serum took on a stickier consistency and Jan braced himself to re-test it. He went outside in search of a suitable specimen and came across a dead crow at the roadside, one wing partly crushed by the wheel of a carriage. Its body was still intact so he took it inside and laid it on the table. He made a small incision in the bird's neck and inserted a droplet of serum. A bead of sweat fell from his forehead into the open wound.

"Drat!" he cursed, fearful it might contaminate the mixture. But, as he leaned on the work bench, head in hands, wondering how to repair this damage, Jan heard a scratching sound; it was the crow, alive and dragging its claws across the workbench. He gently repositioned it to take pressure off its injured wing. Then, with a steady hand, he stitched up the opening in its neck. All he could do now was watch and wait.

Fig A: Pre Serum

Fig B: Post Serum

A day later, the crow was still alive. Jan's modifications to the serum had been successful. As he waited for Zuzana to arrive, the sun streaming through the shutters, sending warm beams across his face, he thought of Greta and her peahen. He wondered where they were, if they were safe, if he'd ever see her again. But he knew not to dwell too much on such thoughts. He knew it was best to kept as busy as possible, because in these moments spent alone, his mind flooded with thoughts of those he'd lost. His mother and father, his uncle and now perhaps Greta.

So, Jan turned his attention to considering how and when he would increase his serum's impact. He had to test it on mammals next, larger creatures whose anatomy was more akin to humans, and then, finally, on humans themselves. He went to the window. No sign of Zuzana. He looked forward to her visits more than anything, but he could never be sure when she'd come. She had to seize opportunities to steal away whenever they arose. When she wasn't around, Jan got on with his work and by night he visited the House of the Hidden, in case Greta or Ignaz had been sighted there, although as the days passed, his hopes of finding them was beginning to ebb. These days the crone at the door had stopped demanding money to let him cross the threshold. She just waved him on in, as if he were one of the regulars.

Of course, Jan knew he still had some to way go before the alchemists accepted him but one day he would find the right person to reveal his work to. Someone who could give him access to the Emperor's Court and, ultimately, help spread the benefits of his serum. So far, only Zuzana knew about it, and he wasn't ready to trust anyone at the House of the Hidden with his secrets. Not yet.

Just then, he spotted Zuzana passing beneath Tyn Courtyard's eastern archway. As usual, she was swathed in a long hooded cloak, her face partially veiled, but her graceful gait was unmistakable.

"You made it!" he called, running to greet her. "I was beginning to worry you couldn't come today."

"I have the whole afternoon," she smiled, narrowing her eyes and crinkling her nose in the glare of the sun. "My father's busy with work, my brothers are out hunting and my mother's being fitted for a new gown. I won't be missed." She shrugged. "You can help me in the Ghetto, if you're still sure you want to."

"Of course. How else could I hope to become a doctor? A man of medicine must know his patients."

"Then we'll go straight there, but you realise how upsetting it will be, don't you? You mustn't let your shock show. The disease may have made monsters of their bodies, but they're still people."

"I know," said Jan. "I saw what it did to my mother and father."

"Of course." She blushed, brushing back her raven hair. "Forgive me." She took Jan's arm and they left the courtyard and crossed Old Town Square. "How's the crow?"

"Livelier than ever. I'll show you later if there's time. But a crow isn't enough," he said despondently.

"Come on, Jan, you've already achieved what alchemists have sought for centuries."

"But what use is that in itself? At the moment I've done no better than those who claim to transform powder into gold; why create more gold if it's not used to help the poor? What's the point in a mixture that revives a dead bird if it can't also cure the sick? And even if it *could*, what good would it do if no one but you or I knew about it? Who will listen to us?"

"Don't be so hard on yourself," Zuzana said. "You've made

amazing progress. Your uncle would be proud. *I'm* proud. I promised I'd help you bring your work to the attention of the right people and I will. My father has connections. But I can't bother him at the moment. He's not been well. But one day he'll listen. They all will. I'll make sure of it."

"I'm sorry. I hope he gets better soon," Jan replied, leaning close and picking a leaf from her hair.

"He will," she replied, but her eyes betrayed her worry. "We're nearly there now."

She led Jan down an alley just round the corner from the Great Synagogue. "Put this on," said Zuzana, handing Jan a leather mask that covered his mouth and nose. "Don't worry. They're used to seeing me in mine. We have to protect ourselves, from the disease and smell. It will turn your stomach as much as their pain will twist your heart."

Jan did as Zuzana asked, then watched her run to greet a figure a few paces ahead. It was a young woman, skeletally thin, her face prematurely haggard. Zuzana held out a parcel of bread and fruit. "Have you seen them today?" she asked, gesturing to the next house.

The woman shook her matted chestnut hair. "Be careful in there," she warned. "It's a house of phantoms. Even the little one has it now. All cursed. All doomed." She took Zuzana's gift. "Thank you," she said, clutching the food to her sunken chest. "Thank you." Then she scuttled inside. "Mother, we have food! We have food!"

Zuzana tapped on the door of the neighbouring house. "Hello!" she called. "It's me."

They entered what seemed little more than a stable. It was dark, barely furnished, the floor strewn with straw, but it was home to a family; an elderly couple and younger man, all in the advanced stages of the plague. Jan saw how every exposed area of their skin was covered in blistered black swellings that wept and itched. His head began to spin as he relived the moment he'd known his mother and father would never recover. He grasped the doorframe to steady himself, wondering how doctors withstood witnessing such sights each day.

"Morning, Jacob," said Zuzana, her voice muffled through her mask.

The elderly man managed to raise a faint smile. "You're a good girl, Zuzana" he said. "An angel. But I don't know how much longer I can take this. It feels like nails are being driven into my flesh. I don't know how you can bear to touch me."

Jan watched in awe as Zuzana pulled on a thick pair of gloves then tended to the whole family – first the old man, then his wife, then his son-in-law, cleansing their blisters before applying a cooling mint balm to ease the itching. But she also did much more than that. She listened to them, spoke to them, restored their dignity. She lightened their spirits and soothed their minds as much as their bodies.

"Where's Miriam?" she asked.

The old man nodded in the direction of the back room. His eyes filled with tears. "She's not good. Not good at all." With trembling hands he reached out and grasped Zuzana's arm. "Don't worry about me. I'm old and useless; she's just a babe."

"We'll do all we can. Jan, check on her, will you? Apply some of the balm. I'll be along in a moment."

"Who's this?" asked Jacob.

"This is Jan, a very good friend of mine. He'll be a fine doctor one day. We're lucky to have him with us."

"Tell him we're not bad people. We've done nothing to deserve this. I used to be a scholar. I studied with Rabbi Loew. You must know of him? He and I were like brothers. I hear he's persuaded the Emperor to see him, to discuss doing something about the conditions we live in here."

"Of course. Of *course* you don't deserve it," Jan assured him. He went next door and, in the corner of the room, saw a little girl curled up on a heap of rags. She was singing to herself, twisting her ringlets and rocking back and forth in time with the tune.

"Hello," he said.

She looked up at him, wide-eyed. It was the girl he'd seen in the funeral procession. She still had the swellings on her neck, and her face was still mottled with black and blue blotches. Only now there were more growths and the bruising had spread. Jan did his best to stay strong, but it was no good. He turned away for a moment, swallowing hard while he wiped away his tears. Then he set down his sack and knelt beside the girl.

"Where's Mama?" she asked. "I want Mama. And Sam."

"Sam?" asked Jan.

"My brother. My big brother."

"Tell me about him," said Jan softly.

The girl's face lit up. "He was my best friend. He looked after me. We used to go to the river to watch the fishermen. But he's not here any more. Grandfather said he and Mama needed to rest for a long, long time."

"Hush, don't cry. It's better for them that they're resting."

"How do you know that?" she sniffed, scratching the sores on her neck.

"Because the same happened to my mother and father. They've gone too, but so has their pain. Here, I have some ointment to ease the itching."

Zuzana glanced into the room and beckoned Jan. "Do you have any of your elixir with you?" she whispered.

"Of course," he replied. "Always. Why?"

"I wondered about giving some to Miriam. You can see

she doesn't have long."

Jan looked from Zuzana to Miriam. He thought for a moment, rubbed his brow. "No. I can't. I won't. I haven't tried it on humans yet, living or dead."

"But what harm could it do?" Zuzana pleaded. "How much worse could things be for her?"

"Much worse. Imagine if it made her pain more intense, or death come quicker. I can't be responsible for that. I won't risk it. Not yet."

"But what if it didn't make things worse for her? What if it eased her pain awhile?"

"Don't Zuzana, please."

"I understand. Then our work here today is done."

———————————————

They left the Ghetto in silence, Zuzana wondering if Miriam would survive until her next visit, Jan worrying he'd made the wrong decision.

"I'm sorry," he said, breaking the tension. "I'm so sorry, but I just couldn't. She's too small, too fragile."

"Don't," said Zuzana, laying a finger on his lips. "Don't dwell on it. I shouldn't have pressed you. We need to cheer ourselves. What good are we to anyone in this sorry state?"

They spent the rest of the afternoon exploring the city together. They climbed Petrin Hill and meandered around Strahov Monastery, their faces aglow with the warmth of the bright spring sun, the smell of cherry blossom filling their nostrils. Then they crossed to the east bank and followed the river south until they came to the outlying district of Vysehrad, which means High Castle. They ran past the Church of Saints Peter and Paul through the park to the rocky edge overlooking the Vltava River.

"That's Libuse's Bath," said Zuzana, pointing to the ruins

of an ancient castle cut into the cliff face beneath them. "She was Prague's founding queen, the city's mythical mother. Legend says she stood on this very edge, gazed to the north and foresaw a city whose towers would reach to the heavens and whose people would be blessed with great riches."

They were quiet for a moment as they sat watching the afternoon sun cast a pink and purple glow across the sky.

"She was right about the city reaching to the heavens," said Jan, looking at the distant spires of St Vitus's Cathedral, "but not many of its inhabitants are blessed with riches. Don't you think she'd be horrified to see so many poor, sick people? And it's not just here. Think of all the people at risk in other lands too. You'd think the Emperor would do more for his people. You'd think he'd order his physicians to find a cure."

"He is doing something. You heard Jacob. He's in talks with Rabbi Loew."

"That's not enough," Jan snapped.

"I know I haven't lost my parents like you have, but don't you think I share your frustration? Don't you think I feel angry too? I've seen so many good people die, people I've come to know and love. It's unwise to let rage get the better of you. And you shouldn't hinge *everything* on whether you'll get to see the Emperor. Being obsessed with one thing like that has made him a sad, lonely man."

"You're right," Jan agreed, feeling a little calmer, "although I wonder if there's any point trying to get my elixir to the Emperor if people in his court doubt his sanity …"

"What do you mean?" Zuzana interrupted. "Who said that? You can't believe what people say."

"Why do you keep defending him?" Jan came back.

"I don't … I mean I don't want us to argue," said Zuzana, her voice trembling. "I wish I could explain."

"I wish you could too," Jan replied, looking her in the eye. "We're friends, aren't we?"

"Here," said Zuzana, offering Jan a parcel from her basket. "Have something to eat."

"This reminds me of when Mother, Father and I would eat our lunch in the meadows in summertime."

"I can't imagine ever doing something like that with my parents. They're so different from how you describe yours. My father ..."

"What about your father?"

"Nothing. It doesn't matter."

"I've told you everything, but you still seem to hold as many secrets as this city."

Zuzana felt she was being tugged in every direction. "I have to go."

"When will I see you again?" Jan called after her.

"I'm not sure," she replied. "It's hard to say." Then she raced off, faster than the wind that whipped about her.

Jan scrambled to his feet. "Wait!" he yelled.

Jan raced past the Church of Saints Peter and Paul, wove through the woods and caught up with Zuzana outside St Martin's Rotunda.

"I'm sorry," he panted. "We ought never to quarrel. You're all I have. I mean, you're everything I have."

"I'm sorry too," Zuzana said, smiling. "You're everything I have too."

Suddenly, a bolt of panic shot through Jan. "My sack!" he exclaimed. "I must have left it in Miriam's room."

"Then it will be safe," she said, putting her arm through his. "I'll come with you to fetch it before going home."

"Back so soon," Jacob greeted them.

"Only briefly, I'm afraid," said Zuzana. "Jan thinks he may have left his bag here. Have you seen it?"

"Ah yes, Miriam has it. It seems she took quite a liking to you, Jan. She's been looking after it. Go through." Jacob gestured to the door.

Jan went to the next room and found Miriam still singing to herself.

"I like your pretty glass," she said. "Shiny. Tastes like sour berries."

"What glass, Miriam?"

To Jan's horror, she raised a hand and licked the stopper of the elixir bottle.

"No!" he shouted, grabbing it from her.

Her lower lip began to curl.

Zuzana rushed in, followed by Jacob. "What is it?"

"She's had some of the serum. What if ...?" Jan gave an anguished cry and began to pace the room.

"Hush now, Miriam," Zuzana comforted. "Jan didn't mean to shout. How much did you drink?"

"I just tasted it. I didn't know I wasn't supposed to."

"What was in the bottle?" asked Jacob, alarmed by Jan's behaviour. He'd seemed so gentle this afternoon.

"It's a medicine Jan has been developing," Zuzana explained.

"Medicine? So what's all the fuss? Unless ..." Jacob faltered. "Unless it was meant for someone else. Someone who can afford expensive remedies."

"That's not it. You don't understand. It's never been tested on humans. I don't know if it's safe. I'm sorry. I shouldn't have left it here. It was stupid of me." Jan struck his fist against a wall.

"You need to calm yourself," said Zuzana, taking hold of his arms. "Have you even examined Miriam?"

Jan knew she was right, and felt foolish for reacting so angrily. He went to Miriam, inspected her swellings. She wasn't as feverish, and the growths on her neck certainly didn't look any worse. But that didn't prove anything. That might just be the temporary effect of the balm, and he didn't want to give false hope to Miriam's family.

Slowly, Jan raised his head, suddenly aware that all eyes were upon him, awaiting an assessment he wasn't sure he was equipped to make.

"Is your medicine magic?" asked Miriam, breaking the silence.

"I think some magic has been worked this afternoon," said Jacob, shuffling towards Jan. "I don't know what your mixture's made of, lad, but Miriam's been in brighter spirits since your visit."

"I'll do all I can for her, sir," said Jan. "I promise."

They left the cottage in a daze. *This it is it,* Jan thought. *The ultimate test.*

Chapter Thirteen
The Sign of the Silver Bullet

E mperor Rudolf was seated on a throne in Belvedere Palace's central hall. He loosened his pearl-encrusted ruff, grabbed a roasted pheasant leg from the table to his right. He devoured it in seconds, wiped his lips, gulped a mouthful of wine.

"Who's next?" he asked, ready to receive the next hopeful who'd come seeking his patronage. "I'll consider anyone with a genuine gift. Alchemists, astrologers, physicians. Craftsmen who might adorn my chambers with exquisite furnishings, goldsmiths who might fashion me unusual trinkets. Anyone who has something interesting to say, some remarkable skill to demonstrate, regardless of wealth or status. Ability and innovation matter more."

Rudolf had established this weekly event several years ago and it remained one of the few public engagements he enjoyed, a chance to discover brilliant minds to enhance his Empire. The talented were rewarded with roles in his court while the fraudulent were punished with imprisonment, sometimes even torture, in Daliborka Tower. He'd sent three men there this morning. The first had claimed to speak the language of birds, the second had claimed he could convert ice into fine crystal, while the third had attempted to resurrect a stuffed serpent. All had been exposed as charlatans but, despite this, Rudolf remained in good spirits. He'd just had some new items installed in the innermost chamber of his Cabinet of Curiosities – a mechanical iron chair that could be set to restrain whoever sat in it, along with a pair of automaton twins to guard it and a clockwork peacock.

"Who's next?" he repeated, eager to get on. "The sun is high, the sky is clear. The signs are good; there must be someone worthy of my support."

Oswald Croll and Tycho Brahe exchanged knowing looks, wondering what would happen when Rudolf's good humour passed, as it inevitably would. They knew him well. They'd seen it many times; jubilation followed by rage and withdrawal. So, every week at this time Brahe would come down from the astronomical observatory on the first floor of the Belvedere and Croll would leave his surgery, to both keep an eye on Rudolf's health and help him detect any trickery.

Croll checked today's list of attendees. "Next we have a man who claims he can stop bullets in mid flight."

"What are you waiting for?" Rudolf replied. "Have him brought in."

A footman went to the reception area. "Ignaz Muller. Greta Grausam," he called to the group of hopefuls.

"What did I tell you?" Ignaz smirked as he rose from his chair. "I knew we'd be selected. You do remember the plan, don't you?" he said.

"I do," Greta replied, determined not to let anything spoil her first imperial engagement.

For a time she'd feared she'd have to wait months to reach

this point. Her plans had been temporarily thwarted when she'd tried in vain to find success with the sample of elixir she'd taken from Gustav's laboratory. But no matter how she'd persevered, no matter how many plants and insects she'd tried to revive, nothing had had any discernable effect, yet she longed for some *immediate* means of improving her life. So, when Ignaz had revealed his plans for entering the court, Greta had decided he would not go alone.

Dressed in her finest gown – a rippling river of red and gold silk, cinched in at the waist and set off by a finely woven golden headdress – Greta strode down the airy corridor. There was no way Ignaz would outshine her today.

The footman showed them inside and closed the door, leaving Greta gasping at the hall's splendour. The floor was polished marble, the walls cool mint green trimmed with golden borders. And the air was heavy with the scent of exotic flowers. On one side, the room was lined with portraits of the Hapsburg family, including a painting of Rudolf as Vertumnus, Roman god of seasons and growth, gardens and fruit trees, by Arcimboldo, the progressive court artist he'd sat for since childhood.

Greta imagined herself living here, pictured her peahen strutting through the maze and gardens in which the Belvedere Palace was set. It was so peaceful, a world away from the bustle of the city below. It made sense that the gardens and palace had been built by Rudolf's grandfather as a token of love for his wife, Queen Anne. The secret grottos with their statues, rambling roses and dazzling tulips – the first to be grown in Europe – would make perfect hideaways, as would the groves of olive, orange, cherry and pomegranate trees, all planted to spell out mystical symbols.

"Come closer," Croll ordered from the far end of the room "And come quick. You have ten minutes."

"Sirs, it's my pleasure and privilege to be here," Ignaz announced with a stiff bow. "Ten minutes is plenty. I'll have proven my worth long before my time is up."

The click-clack of his polished knee-high boots echoed round the hall as he strode towards Croll, Brahe and the stooped figure of the Emperor. He opened his case. "You can see this is a perfectly ordinary piece of shooting equipment and this, an ordinary solid silver bullet. Please, inspect them."

While Croll examined the equipment, Greta positioned herself across the room.

"Everything seems to be in order."

"Naturally," Ignaz replied, sticking to his tactic of behaving as though he belonged here, in the Emperor's court. He took the gun and loaded it. "Behold the transformation of silver into air."

He released the trigger and the bullet raced towards Greta. The room turned cold with tension. Then, a split second before it lodged itself between her eyes, it vanished into thin air.

"Behold the transformation of air into gold dust," Ignaz announced, crossing the room and grasping the air at the point the bullet had disappeared. He opened his hand to reveal a mound of glittering powder. "Have this tested, if you like," he suggested, sprinkling it onto the table, next to a platter of greasy bones.

"Explain your methods," demanded Brahe.

"You know I can never do that," said Ignaz with a wry smile, "but I'm sure you can envisage how useful my talent might be. Imagine a whole battalion of alchemist soldiers who could make the enemy's weapons disappear."

"Offer him a position," ordered Rudolf. "Frederick needs someone."

Brahe nodded. "That's settled. You'll take up residence with Duke Frederick of Stuttgart and we'll monitor your progress under his tutelage. If you prove yourself there, you might, one day, join the court here."

"With respect," said Ignaz, "and grateful as I am for this opportunity, I have no wish to move to Germany."

"Is that so?" snapped Croll. He had little time for self-importance. "A scientist must be a traveller, an explorer. Knowledge comes from experience. I journeyed throughout the continent – Germany, France, Switzerland – before coming here, all the while studying and learning. The path to enlightenment is never linear. But," he continued, more anxious to return to his work than to prolong this discussion, "as it happens, you won't be going to Stuttgart. You'll be based in the Duke's Bohemian estate in the town of Kutna Hora, three hours by coach to the southeast of Prague. He's a reputable patron of Natural Magic, with a fine library and associations with all the great alchemists."

"I know of him," said Greta. "My late husband, a scientist, said he was a respectable amateur alchemist."

"Come closer," the Emperor called to Greta. "You strike me as possessing an unusual degree of wit for a woman. And such composure too, a fearless spirit. Not so much as a blink even as the bullet raced towards you."

Physically, he was one of the most repulsive men she'd ever seen but, behind the stare of his melancholic eyes Greta saw something strangely charismatic. She went to him, curtsied low. The Emperor took her hands and laid his lips on them.

"It's my pleasure to meet you," he said. "Tell me, who was your husband?"

"Gustav Grausam, of Vienna. He'd been working on an

Elixir of Life before his death. I learned many things from his library and laboratory. He had a fine collection of rare plants and animal specimens. He even made a new species of bird, and –"

"We should make arrangements for your move to the Duke's estate," Croll interrupted, aware that time was pressing on and the Emperor had other matters to attend to.

"Kutna Hora," he went on. "The name means 'Mountain of the Monk's Cowl'. Silver is so plentiful there that it virtually springs from the earth like water. If you've ever supped from a silver goblet, chances are the raw material was mined in Kutna Hora. As for the Duke, he's the most powerful man in the region; law enforcer, tax collector, owner of one of the finest collections of alchemical texts in all Bohemia. We shall send a carriage to collect you tonight."

"Thank you for this opportunity. We shan't disappoint you," Ignaz promised.

"Yes, thank you," said Greta, fixing her eyes on the Emperor.

With that, they left the Belvedere. "I'll be back soon," Ignaz muttered under his breath. "This is only the start. One day I'll be given a whole suite of rooms here in the castle." He turned to Greta. "I'll be along later to pack. I shall go directly to the House of the Hidden to make it known that Ignaz Muller's star is rising."

Greta said nothing. She felt certain her own star was also rising, certain this wouldn't be her only encounter with the Emperor, for hadn't she ignited a spark in his miserable soul? She was certain she had.

───────── ◆ ─────────

"Not a bad morning's work," Croll remarked once they were alone again in the hall. "I think the Duke will make good use of Muller, and he'll keep his brashness in check too."

"What's that?" barked Rudolf, rising from his throne. "It's far too hot in here. Open the windows, all of them," he wheezed. "I can't breathe. Let me out. I need air." He tore off his ruff, pushed past Croll and Brahe and stumbled out to the gardens.

"As your physician, I advise you to lie down," called Croll. "You're burning up."

"And as the Holy Roman Emperor I advise you to mind your own damn business. Help me to the carriage," he ordered a footman waiting outside the Belvedere. "I have to get away. I don't care where to. Just drive."

But Rudolf felt no better for leaving the confines of his court amidst the clatter of sixteen newly-shod hooves. Heart hammering, forehead sodden with salty sweat, he couldn't believe what he was seeing. He rubbed his streaming eyes but nothing changed. They were still there. The mechanical people who seemed as artificial as the objects in his Cabinet of Curiosities. Except these were supposed to be real people, going about their daily business on the streets of Prague. This was his worst fit yet.

"Make it stop!" he cried, covering his ears, convinced he could hear their joints creak and screech and grind as if they were made of iron, jerking and juddering like monstrous semi-human counterparts of themselves. Everywhere he looked he saw a grotesque version of the world populated not by humans but by automatons.

"Damnation! What now?" cursed the driver as they turned onto Charles Bridge. If it wasn't enough to hear his master raving behind him, he could see a large crowd of darkly-clad people ahead, fast approaching from the east bank. There must have been over a hundred of them. There wasn't enough room to pass and they clearly weren't going to move but before the footman had a chance to tug on the reins, the horses stopped of their own accord.

Rudolf banged on the ceiling. "Keep going, fool!"

"I can't, sir. There's some kind of disturbance ahead."

Rudolf struggled down from the carriage and watched as Rabbi Loew stretched out on the ground. His followers reached into their pockets and pelted him with clods of clay that transformed into rose petals and violets as they made contact with him. He was soon buried beneath a blanket of blossoms.

"See how the grime from the banks of the Vltava River can be transformed," Loew called, his voice ringing out above the rush of the river's waters as he lifted himself to his feet. "And so it can be in other matters. Where there is death, there can be life; where there is disease, there can be health."

Turning to face the Emperor he continued. "We were on our way to see you, to urge you to do something about the plight of the people in the Ghetto. At our first meeting I asked for immediate action, yet you've done nothing while Death continues to stalk the streets, stealing the souls of our children as they sleep. We're running out of fingers to close their eyes, voices to bless their souls, hands to dig their graves. Poisonous fumes from their unburied bodies contaminate the alleys, and the ghosts of those who have been buried rise nightly. Their tiny forms dance above their tombstones, an agonising reminder that we've failed them.

"Your Majesty, I repeat: order your court physicians to heal your subjects and work to find a cure. It's your duty to purge this sickness from your lands."

The footman shifted nervously, exchanging an uneasy glance with the driver. No one had ever dared speak to the Emperor like this. But then, rather than issue punishment,

Rudolf took hold of Loew's hands and shook them as if he were an old friend.

"I respect you. I value your wisdom and courage. And you're real, too. You have skin and blood and bones. You're not one of *them*."

"One of who?" asked Loew, alarmed at how unstable a condition the Emperor was in. "Please, let me escort you home, or send for your physician."

"I mean you're *real*, not one of the half-humans I've seen roaming the city. The winged-women, the iron men. You must understand, you made a Man of Clay, didn't you?"

"I did," replied Loew. "But I see no winged-women or iron men."

"No one does but me," Rudolf murmured. "No one."

He gathered his thoughts. "It's obvious Fate brought us together here today, in this precise location. The first stone of this bridge was laid by my ancestor in the most auspicious of circumstances, during an unusual alignment of Saturn and the sun. I know I failed to take action before, but our chance conjunction here today is a sign from the heavens. I shall order my best physicians to turn their attention to this immediately. You have my word."

"Thank you. I don't need to tell you what this might mean for the future of the people of this city, and beyond."

But the wise man's joy was tinged with concern for Rudolf's state of mind. And the wise man wondered how much truth there might be in his ravings.

Alone in a lodging house to the north of the city, Greta sat transfixed in front of a mirror, pondering the day that had passed and the future that might follow. She wasn't sure how much more she could take of Ignaz's arrogance. But, she had to admit that few could have secured a position within such an illustrious household in so short a time. Ignaz was nothing if not charming when the need arose.

So, she would go with him to Duke Frederick's estate, for isn't this what she'd always wanted? Elevation to the higher realms of society. This position might be the stepping stone she needed, although her sights remained firmly fixed on greater things. Like the marvel of *real* magick, and the rewards it might bring. She was mystified as to why the elixir had completely failed her, wondered if Jan was having more success with it, if he'd managed to find an apprenticeship in the five or six weeks they'd been in Prague. Gustav's experiment to lengthen the lifespan of butterflies had certainly worked. There they were, flickering fast and bright in a jar on the dressing table. Normal butterflies would have died months ago.

But there was no time to ponder further. There was still packing to be done. Greta pulled a casket from beneath the bed. Inside were three rows of nut-encased peahen eggs, each sealed with her blood and a single indigo and emerald feather.

> *"Your shells are earth, your whites are water*
> *Your membrane is air, your yolks are fire, and gold:*
> *The heart of everything.*
> *Your wholes are as heaven*
> *Protecting life, cultivating immortality"*

she chanted. Then, slowly and carefully, she opened a separate compartment in the casket and looked inside. All at once the creatures within began to flap their wings and squawk and scratch, releasing a flurry of feathers and hair.

"You'll soon be too big for this box, won't you my

beauties? I shall have to find you a new home."

Just then, Greta heard the click of Ignaz's heels on the stairs. She closed the casket, concealed it in a trunk she'd packed for the journey and went to the door to greet him.

"How did you find the House of the Hidden?" she asked. "Did you tell people our news?"

"Naturally, and I learned this evening that Duke Frederick is more respected and wealthy than I'd hoped."

"Very good," said Greta, smoothing down her skirts. "I must finish packing. The carriage will be here within the hour. Come with me, my beauty."

The peahen cocked its head and strutted off behind its mistress.

Chapter Fourteen
Death and the Rose

It was almost ten o'clock and dark by the time Jan left the Place of the Black Bear, but the night felt almost as humid as day. Tyn Courtyard was packed with traders sitting on benches beneath the cherry trees. There was an energy in the air and Jan would have liked to have joined them, but he had to make his nightly pilgrimage to the House of the Hidden.

Jan found the inn eerily silent. There was no lively debate, no clinking of goblets or clashing of tankards. No demonstrations of transformations. Instead, Jan saw several groups of stony-faced men.

"I can't believe it," said one, shaking his head. "It's a tragedy for the people of the Ghetto. No, for the whole city. And just when he'd persuaded the Emperor to do something about the plague."

At that word, Jan flinched. He thought of Miriam. What would they find when they visited her next morning?

"His death is a tragedy indeed," the conversation

continued around him. He edged nearer. "An achievement on Loew's behalf, granted, but I'm not sure how much faith we should store in the Emperor's promise," came another voice. "Everyone knows he's a broken man, half-deranged, while Loew had made a death-defying device."

"In that case, how did he die?" said a third man.

"He died because where loved ones are involved, we're all weak, even someone with Loew's intelligence. Come close and listen, for I promise you will never have heard the like of this before, and I swear you will never hear such a thing again."

Jan drew closer still. What did it mean that the great Loew had died?

"As you know, Rabbi Loew had spent a great many hours studying the plague that feeds on our people like a starved dog, but the cause and cure of this pestilence that surges through our streets like a river of poisoned blood constantly evaded him. That is, until recently, when Loew thought he'd found a way to drive Death from all our doors.

"A few weeks ago, in the dead of night, Loew remembered he'd left some important papers in the synagogue so he returned to his place of work. As he stood outside the cemetery gates an ashen figure appeared before him. There was no doubt in his mind. Loew knew that this apparition was Death. And in his bony hand Death held a long list of names; people who would fall victim to the plague the next day. Loew's name and the names of many of his friends and neighbours were on this list. Without thinking, Loew snatched it from Death's clutch and tore it into tiny pieces, knowing that while he had escaped on this occasion, from now on, wherever he was and whatever he did, Death would be waiting to claim him. So he created a small mechanical device that tinkled whenever Death was at hand."

"What kind of device?" asked another man. "How did it work?"

"I cannot answer that, for I am not so wise as he. But on with the story. A few days later, when he was on his way to the synagogue Loew was approached by a smart-looking gentleman. As the man came close, Loew's machine began to tinkle. The man's cloak fell from his shoulders and exposed his skeletal form and Loew escaped Death a second time.

"Then, only a few days ago, on his way to this very inn, Loew was hailed by an elderly tradeswoman. As she neared Loew, his device began to tinkle and all at once the old woman's walking stick became a scythe and her scarf slipped from her head to reveal a naked skull. And so Loew escaped Death a third time.

"But yesterday, on the occasion of his birthday, Loew was so overwhelmed by the affection of his friends and family that he left his device in his study. His granddaughter presented him with a gift of a rose and as soon as he smelled it Loew dropped to the floor and died. Death had been hiding in the rose."

Jan wasn't sure what to think. Did this make it less likely Rudolf would do anything to stop the plague? He checked his watch. Almost midnight. He knew he should get some sleep – Zuzana was coming early tomorrow – but as he opened the door to leave the House of the Hidden he felt something grasp his arm.

"He was here again tonight," cackled the crone.

"Who?" asked Jan, wishing she'd release her bony grip.

"Ignaz Muller. But you missed him. He left a few hours ago. Said he had to go and pack. He's been offered a fancy position outside the city. He's taking that new lady of his with him. Said they were leaving tonight."

"Tonight? Did he say where they were going?" Jan asked.

He shifted from foot to foot, not sure what to think. He was glad to know Greta was well, but shocked to hear she was leaving Prague. Had she given up hope of finding him?

"Elishka," she called to the serving girl, "did you hear where Muller was heading?"

"Ignaz? That slimy pig?" she spat. "I heard him boasting about being offered a job with some duke. Duke Frederick, that's it. Lives in a town called Kutna Hora, next to the main church there. I hope he never comes back."

"Why's that?" asked Jan.

"Because he's a swindler, that's why. He's a barber by trade, knows as much about alchemy as I do. He'll take your aunt for every penny she's got and then abandon her. I've seen it before. I'd be very worried if she were my aunt."

Chapter Fifteen
The Parting and the Promise

"What do you mean you're leaving Prague?" asked Zuzana. "Would you have gone without telling me?"

Jan sighed, long and deep. It hurt him to see Zuzana like this. He'd spent all night agonising as to whether this was the right thing to do. He didn't want to leave her, and he knew he had a responsibility to check on Miriam. But he also had a duty to see Greta was all right; Gustav would have wanted him to.

"Please don't be angry. I'll be back as soon as I can, but I have to go. Greta might be in danger."

"What kind of danger?"

"I'm not sure exactly. I heard she's gone to Kutna Hora with the man we met when we first arrived here. People say he's a fraudster."

"I couldn't bear anything to happen to you," said Zuzana.

"I'll look after myself. I'll have to." Jan looked her in the eye. "You could always come with me."

"You know I can't. I'd love to but ... my family. And what about Miriam? We were supposed to go there this morning. Can't you at least wait until we've done that?"

"I wish I could, but a tradesman has offered me a lift. He's waiting on Old Town Square."

"But how will you even find her there? It's not a small town."

"Don't worry. I know exactly where she's staying. The Emperor gave them a position with a duke there. I'll miss you," he said, squeezing Zuzana's hand. Then he picked up his bag and strode across the courtyard.

"I'll miss you too," Zuzana called after him. "Very much."

Zuzana didn't care who saw her return home that morning. She had other things on her mind, more important things.

After Jan had gone she'd sat awhile in the House of the Black Bear trying to excuse him for having departed so suddenly. She leafed through the papers he'd left strewn across the table, ran a hand across his work robes, and realised she was being selfish, that although she didn't feel very close to them, she would do the same for her family, even her brothers, if they were in trouble. *He'll be back soon. I know he will,* she told herself.

Then she'd gone to the Ghetto and found Miriam in good spirits. She was eating properly for the first time in weeks and the swellings on her neck were no worse, which was a good sign, for they'd been spreading swiftly these past few days.

Of course, this didn't mean she was cured, that the fever wouldn't return, but she was definitely in less pain.

If only you could have waited another hour, Zuzana thought. *Then you'd have seen for yourself. And we could have gone to my father's physicians with proof that the serum might work.*

Back in her room, she sank onto the bed. "I was going to tell you," she wept. "I wanted to tell you all along. The Emperor. He's my father."

This was the secret – the only secret – she'd kept from Jan, for she knew if word got out that the Emperor's daughter had been seen gallivanting around the city, unchaperoned, day and night, she would have been sent away in disgrace. She'd already been caught once. Croll had seen her sneaking into the castle and, after initially threatening to tell her father, when she'd revealed where she'd been and why, he'd been persuaded to keep quiet. "On the understanding that this won't happen again," he'd said.

Next time I see you, I'll tell you everything, she promised. It was all too much. She cried so hard her head hurt and eventually fell into a dream of a tale she'd been told as a child.

Beautiful Verushka whose Fear Failed her Love

There was once a beautiful girl named Verushka and a handsome boy named Radek who were fonder of each other than anything. They spent their days together and their nights dreaming of one another. But then the day came when war broke out and Radek had to go off to fight and leave sweet Verushka behind. Before he went, he asked her to wait for him for seven years and seven weeks and then they would be married.

When the war ended all the boys and men began to return home to their families and loves. Verushka heard news of this and went outside to wait for Radek. By nightfall he still hadn't come so she went to bed and dreamed of his homecoming. But there was no sign of him the next day, nor the next, nor the next. After a whole week Radek still hadn't arrived and Verushka's eyes were sore and red from all her crying.

After some months had passed, Verushka began to receive marriage proposals from many young men but she refused them all, saying, "I will wait for my Radek until my dying day."

But then after seven years and seven weeks had passed and there was still no sign of Radek, Verushka wondered

what she should do, thinking how terrible it would be if Radek returned after she'd accepted a proposal from someone else, but also thinking it would be terrible if she refused all the proposals and he never returned. So Verushka went to the village wise woman to seek her advice.

The old woman listened carefully to Verushka's troubles then asked, "Do you love him?"

"More than anything," Verushka replied.

"Then the answer is simple," said the wise woman. "In the far right-hand corner of the old cemetery, next to the great oak tree, you will find a human rib bone. Take this bone, then go to the river and fill a pot with water. Add in three handfuls of silt and place the pot in an oven for the whole afternoon. Remove it and add a scattering of grain until the mixture is thick as porridge. Finally, you should stir it with the bone from eleven until midnight. Then, no matter where he's lying in the cold, dark earth, your love will come to you."

So Verushka did exactly as the wise woman instructed. She went to the far right-hand corner of the old cemetery, and there, next to the great oak tree, she found the human rib. Then she went to the river, filled a pot with water and scooped in three handfuls of silt. She heated the pot in her oven for the whole afternoon then scattered in some grain until the mixture became as thick as porridge. Finally, at eleven o'clock, she took the bone and began to stir. Suddenly a voice came from the pot saying, "Return, Radek, return."

And Radek heard the voice from his grave many lands away. He sprang from the earth, mounted a white horse and followed the voice all the way to his sweetheart's door.

Verushka ran outside to meet him as the wind howled around them and the rain poured down upon them.

"My love!" she cried. "How long I've waited! Come inside."

But Radek simply took her hands and said, "Collect your things, my sweet, for we must leave right away. I must return to where I was buried before daybreak."

So Verushka packed a bag and went with him, into the cold and stormy night. The white horse took flight so they raced across the skies quick as any bird.

Radek turned to his love and said,

"The moon it shines, my spirit flies
The stars they shine, for my soul they pine.
Sweet Verushka, are you afraid?"

Verushka turned to her love and said, "No, dear Radek, I am not, for we are together." And a shiver ran through her.

They continued over mountains and above fields and lakes, all the while the winds howling and the rain lashing. Radek turned to his love again and shouted above the storm,

> "The moon it shines, my spirit flies
> The stars they shine, for my soul they pine.
> Sweet Verushka, are you afraid?"

Verushka took her love's hand and said, "No, dear Radek, I am not, for we are together." And her heart fluttered like the wings of a little bird.

They flew on, faster and faster, the tempest growing fiercer and fiercer and Radek turned to his love a third time and called,

> "The moon it shines, my spirit flies
> The stars they shine, for my soul they pine.
> Sweet Verushka, are you afraid?"

Verushka laid her head on his shoulder and said, "No, dear Radek, I am not, for I am with you." And her whole body began to tremble as if she were a leaf.

Then they came to a cemetery and the horse returned to the ground and vanished beneath them. Radek led his love to an open grave, saying, "Lie down, my sweet, in the earthen bed you called me from."

"I will," Verushka replied, "but after you."

So Radek jumped into the grave and Verushka threw down her bags after him. Then she turned and ran as fast as she could, for however much she loved Radek, she couldn't bring herself to jump into a grave. She ran and

ran until she could run no more but while she was resting, Verushka heard the stamp of a horse's hooves so she ran off again. Soon she came to a small cottage. She went inside and locked the door behind her. When her eyes had adjusted to the darkness, she realised she wasn't alone for there, stretched out on a table, was the cold corpse of a man who'd once been a sorcerer. Once she'd calmed herself, Verushka curled up in a corner of the room next to the stove.

Just then Radek came riding up to the cottage on the white horse. "Let the dead open the door for the dead who has come for the living," he called.

And the corpse shifted on the table and said, "Give me a moment to move my arm."

Verushka's blood ran cold, for the voice of the corpse was the same as the voice of her love.

Radek called again, "Let the dead open the door for the dead who has come for the living."

And the corpse said, "Give me a moment to move my leg."

Radek called out a third time, "Let the dead open the door for the dead who has come for the living."

And the corpse said, "Give me a moment to move my head." The corpse raised its head, sat up and began to lumber towards the door.

Verushka looked out from the stove and saw the corpse coming towards her with Radek behind him. Just as it was about to lay its hands on her, the cock crowed and both the corpse and handsome Radek collapsed on the floor.

"My love!" called Verushka. "What have I done? I should never have left you!" With that, she also collapsed and died of a broken heart. The very next day she was buried in the grave with Radek.

Zuzana cried out in her sleep. She sat up, vowing to do anything for Jan, and to never let fear hold her back.

"I shall tell Croll everything," she resolved. "I shall take him to Miriam so he can see the miracle of Jan's serum for himself."

There was a knock at the door.

"What is it?" called Zuzana.

"May I come in?" It was her lady-in-waiting. "I'm afraid I bring bad news. It's your brother."

THE THIRD CHAMBER

Artificialia, Curiosa

and Automata

Chapter Sixteen

The Blood of the Hanged in the Village of Bones

"This is where we part," said the tradesman, pulling his horses to a halt.

"Sedlec?" said Jan, noticing the sign at the side of the track.

"Kutna Hora is only a few miles away. You can walk from here."

Jan paid the man a few coins, thanked him for the favour and jumped down from the cart. He walked awhile through the quiet village, wondering which road to take. There was no one about to ask, and it was silent too. No neighing of horses, no birdsong. The evening sky was sprinkled with stars and Jan was reminded of the night he and Gustav had buried the mandrake in Vienna.

Am I any closer to doing what we set out to do?

Jan realised that despite all the setbacks, he was: the elixir had revived a dead bird, he'd begun to make himself known among Prague's alchemical elite. He would just have to wait for news of Miriam's condition.

A large drop of rain landed on his cheek. And then it

began: an almighty rumble of thunder was followed by the opening of the skies. Jan turned up his collar and looked for somewhere to shelter. He ran down the path to a chapel but, as he drew near, he saw this was no ordinary chapel.

Above its arched entrance was a coat of arms fashioned from bones; a shield of skulls formed its outer edge, leg bones made a cross at its centre.

Hesitantly, Jan descended the steps to the lower chamber. The door blew shut behind him, sending a chill through the room. Overhead, something creaked. He looked up and saw a large chandelier swaying back and forth, back and forth, casting jagged shadows across the floor. How many people's bones had been used to make it? It was made of battered skulls, curved ribs, chipped kneecaps, collarbones, all bound together by thin wire to form a hanging tower of death.

To his left, to his right, behind and before him: floor to ceiling arrangements of bones, bones and more bones – there must have been thousands of them – embedded in every alcove, protruding from every wall.

He crept down the steps, cobwebs tickling his cheeks like soft, fleshy fingers, and went to the table of candles. He lit one for his mother, one for his father and one for Gustav. Then he lit a fourth for all the people whose remains were exhibited here. As their light grew, he noticed a plaque nailed to a wall. Jan didn't much want to spend the night here among all these bones, but the rain still lashed and the wind still howled so he found a dry spot in a corner of

BLESSED BE THE SOULS OF
THOSE WHO FELL PREY TO
THE OUTBREAK OF THE PLAGUE
SEDLEC, 1318
THE DOOR TO THIS HOUSE
OF THE DEAD SHALL
ALWAYS BE OPEN

the lower crypt; he would hasten to Kutna Hora first thing in the morning. But no sooner had he settled down on the hard floor and closed his eyes, Jan fell into a fitful dream.

The Curse of Krumlov Castle

*T*ucked into a curve of a fast flowing river was a peaceful looking village named Krumlov, which means Place of the Crooked Meadow. And at the heart of this village was a castle capped by a tall thin tower.

Through a haze, Jan saw the fleshy face of the nobleman who lived there. His eyes burned with rage. His lips were thick, his brow was heavy. Jan thought of the Emperor. But this couldn't be him. The man was too young and stomped too quickly through the castle.

Then came a glint of silver light as the man raised his right hand.

In a flash, Jan saw a young woman appear in the turret. She was shrouded in swirling mists and though her mouth moved, no sound came from her lips. A white fur cape was wrapped around her shoulders. Dark hair flowed down her back. Jan's heart skipped a beat. Could it be Zuzana? Then the mists lifted and he saw it was someone else.

A bulky figure emerged from the shadows and took a knife to the girl. Jan cried out as the man sliced off her pretty head. He winced as her body was hurled from the tower. He held his breath as six guards dressed in the livery of the Royal Court stormed the tower and seized the murderer. Next thing Jan saw was the man haemorrhaging to death in a bath of his own blood.

Jan sat up, shivering in a cold sweat. He glanced around the crypt. Though their sockets were empty, Jan felt he was being watched by the eyes of a thousand grinning skulls.

The rain lashed down hard on Kutna Hora all through the night. Flattening flowers, bowing branches, irritating Greta. It had woken her before dawn and now, as noon approached, it showed no signs of letting up. She looked out on Duke Frederick's landscaped grounds, gazed at the Gothic grandeur of St Barbara's Church.

"Greta!" Ignaz barked. "When are you going to join me in the laboratory? I need your help. I hardly slept last night, what with the rain and constant shrieking of your blasted bird. Anyone would think you had a whole flock of them."

"I'll come when I'm ready," Greta replied. "And not before."

"Good morning," said Duke Frederick, striding into the room. He was lanky, with a pointed nose and a manner so abrupt that conversations with him left people feeling as if they'd been prodded with a sharp stick. "I wanted to let you know a distinguished guest will be arriving shortly, a certain Michael Sendiv."

"Michael Sendiv? The Michael Sendiv?" gasped Greta. "The chemist who turns quicksilver to gold?"

"That's right," confirmed the Duke. "He's come from Prague to demonstrate this very transformation."

"How opportune," said Greta. "I very much look forward to meeting him."

Greta had the esteemed Sendiv under her spell from the moment they met and, while he may have been old and frail, his wits were quick as ever and she was delighted that such a distinguished gentleman seemed interested in her. He listened to her talk about her husband's work and her hopes for the future. And she listened to tales of his travels and discoveries.

"The essence of my new book can be distilled to three rules," he explained. "First, scientists should follow nature's example. Second, scientists should only mix things which are alike. Third, the true meaning of science is incomprehensible to the arrogant. I'm sure your husband would have agreed. I've shared correspondence with his colleagues – Paracelsus, for example – but I'm sorry I never had the pleasure of meeting him. I think we would have had much to talk about, but then so do we, my dear. It's not often one can converse so freely with women."

"Not all men are so enlightened," Greta replied, casting Ignaz a stony glance.

"So, when are we to witness your talents?" asked Ignaz.

"Whenever you like. I'm used to singing for my supper," Sendiv said. "When I worked in Prague I was frequently asked to concoct amulets and tinctures at odd hours. Three, four, five in the morning, whenever the call came, I'd rise from bed to grind bats' bones, or extract sap from exotic plants – whatever the situation demanded – while the Emperor waited and watched."

"The Emperor?" said Ignaz and Greta in unison.

"Yes, I've spent the past few years as one of his chief advisors. Here," he said, holding up the gold medal hanging from the chain around his neck. "Rudolf awarded this to me for my services to science. Now, shall we proceed with the transformation? The hour is late and my bones are weary."

"As you wish," replied the Duke. "This way."

Even with the aid of his ivory cane, Sendiv found walking painful. With each slow, unsteady step he took towards the room at the back of the house, it felt as though his knee joints were grinding themselves down.

"I wasn't always this way, you know," he said as they reached the room. "I was once in perfect physical condition but age has a cruel way of creeping up on you." He fumbled in his pockets and pulled out a drawstring bag and a sealed pot. He emptied a few grains of powder from the bag into a metal dish. It was so vivid, so intensely coloured, that it looked like the very essence of red.

"So, this is the mysterious substance I've heard so much about," said the Duke. "Will you ever disclose its properties?"

"Not in my lifetime," replied Sendiv. "I trust my secrets to no one." He poured a measure of quicksilver from the pot. "Would you mind securing the dish onto the tripod and lighting a candle beneath it, my dear?" he asked. "My hand's not as steady as it was, though my brain's never been steadier. It never stops. I hardly sleep for all the thoughts that fly through it."

Greta did as he asked and they gathered round the table, silent as snowfall, bodies taut as twine, eyes fixed on the mixture.

After a few minutes, and faintly at first, a curious aroma burned their nostrils; the smell of singed hair mixed with earth. It rose in wisps of crimson smoke that swirled above their heads. Greta looked up and, through the haze, saw their shadows flicker fast across the ceiling. She watched her long, thin spectral silhouette loom over Ignaz and Sendiv until the brew began to hiss, and spit lumps of hardened silver pebbles across the table. The smoke cleared and Greta peered into the dish. "I can see it!" she cried. "The transformation has worked!"

And so it had. Where once there'd been scarlet and silver was now a nugget of solid gold.

"For you," said Sendiv, handing it to Greta.

The clock in the hall struck two. A black-clad figure skulked by the staircase, sleek and silent as a prowling cat. It slipped into Sendiv's room and, though it was dark, a strip of moonlight revealed all that the figure needed to see. It pocketed the old man's medal and transformative powder but, as it went to leave, knocked into a dresser.

The old alchemist stirred. "Who's there?"

The figure froze, looked about the room. It picked up a candlestick, struck the chemist on his skull and fled, faster than lightning.

Sendiv cried out.

A servant came rushing to the room.

"Wake the household. Fetch the Duke!"

The servant did as he was asked and, moments later, the Duke himself arrived.

"What's going on? Dear lord! You're bleeding. Did you fall?"

The old man reached out. "My powder! My chain! They've been stolen."

Greta appeared in the doorway, hair tousled from sleep.

"What's happened? Are you all right?" she asked. She found a handkerchief and, kneeling at Sendiv's bedside, pressed it to his wound to stop the flow of blood.

"What's this?" she asked, picking something from the floor.

It was a ring: a circle of bone decorated with a silver ram's head.

"Ignaz," she gasped. "This belongs to him!"

"Are you sure?" asked the Duke. "Could he have done this? Sendiv, did you see anyone?"

"I was asleep. It happened so quickly."

"There's no sign of forced entry, sir," said the servant, "so it can't have been an intruder."

"Check his room. He shall be severely punished, if he hasn't already fled."

Jan was filled with trepidation as he left the House of Bones next morning. With the dreadful apparitions of the night before lingering still, he tramped through the driving rain. They'd seemed so real. He tried to focus his mind, for he still didn't know what he would do when he reached Kutna Hora, when he found Greta. If he found her.

After walking for just over an hour, Jan saw a large church and knew he must be close.

"Excuse me," he asked a passer-by. "I'm looking for Duke Frederick's estate. Do you know where it is?"

"It's right there," she said. "But you're too late. You've missed the hanging."

"Hanging?" said Jan, horrified. "What hanging?"

"You haven't heard? Someone attacked and robbed the Duke's guest, a famous Polish chemist. The culprit's been hanged. He was new to the Duke's staff, a man from Prague who'd claimed to have alchemical powers. Such scandal!" she sniffed. "You only just missed it, mind; his body's still twitching. A handsome reward's been offered to whoever finds the chemist's stolen golden chain and magic powder. Strange times we live in," the woman went on. "Terrible times. Attacks on old alchemists! Murder in the House of the Hapsburgs! But I suppose it's not such a surprise. From the day he was born they said his blood was bad. He's better off dead."

"Murder?" asked Jan. "What happened? Who's dead?"

"Don Julius d'Austria, the Emperor's eldest son, and favourite child by all accounts. The boy was a beast; murdered some young girl in his countryside castle. He deserved nothing better than bleeding to death in his own bath."

"No! That can't be right!" Jan muttered, stumbling backwards. "That can't be right!"

"I'm as sure as bones are bones and flesh is flesh."

Head still spinning, Jan pushed his way through the crowd until he came to the manor's gates.

"Can I help you?" came a stern voice. It was one of the Duke's staff. "You're trespassing," he said, eyeing Jan's dishevelled appearance.

"I'm looking for my aunt," said Jan, smoothing down his hair. "She came here with the man who was hanged. I believe the Duke had taken them into his household."

"She's left for Prague. Now go. You have no business here."

The crowd had dispersed by the time Jan re-crossed the courtyard. He stopped at the sight of Ignaz's body dangling dead. He glanced back one last time before stepping onto the street. Someone slipped towards the gallows and slid a glinting knife from beneath an emerald cloak. A gloved hand reached up, slit Ignaz's torso and filled a vial with the gushing blood.

Chapter Seventeen

The Sign of the Lion, the Child of the World

Clouds had gathered over Prague Castle, but the tempests that raged within the Emperor were darker still. Sitting in a grotto in the Royal Gardens, he was beside himself with despair; he'd just been informed his lion was seriously ill. He caught sight of himself in the mirrors he'd had set into the trees there.

"Then that's it," he addressed his reflection. "My time is up. First my son. Next me, for my fate is as the lion's. I've failed as a father as well as a ruler. What does anything matter?"

Rudolf walked through the grounds, mumbling aloud as he crossed Deer Moat, and breathing heavily for his bulk meant walking took great effort.

"This is still my city," he said, trying to compose himself as he came to the castle walls. "The finest in the world, and no one can take that away from me."

As he looked over the walls to the centre of Prague, Rudolf saw a hulking cloud rise from the muddy depths of the Vltava River, and skeletons jigging above the Ghetto. He rubbed his eyes, in case they'd deceived him. When he looked again he saw neither the cloud nor the skeletons, but a winged creature – half woman, half bird – hovering over Charles Bridge. He watched it glide downstream, wind this way and that as it swooped across the surface of the water.

"Do you see it?" he roared. "Do you see the beast?"

But there was no one to answer his question, no one to assure him it wasn't really there, no one to confirm it was. He fled through fruit groves towards his Cabinet of Curiosities. But, even as he entered the first chamber, *Naturalia*, he knew something wasn't right. He stopped dead. His eyes darted from object to animal – preserved armadillos, pelicans, iguanas and tropical frogs; whale jaws, rhinoceros horns, tiger teeth. He sensed movement and life in every cabinet and case.

Something clattered behind him. He saw drawers of carefully arranged fossils and gemstones, snail and sea-shells opening and closing, opening and closing. Then his collection of rare bird and reptile eggs began to crack. The embryos in jars unfurled. A pair of stuffed hares twitched their noses. The monkey skeletons hanging from the ceiling danced like crazed marionettes. The mandrake root reclining on a velvet cushion stretched its wispy arms into the neck of the glass bottle it was displayed in.

Rudolf supposed his mind was playing tricks on him, supposed he was imagining things. He'd hardly slept a wink since Don Julius's death.

Shakily, he moved to the next chamber, *Scientifica*, and in a room filled with hundreds of timepieces, he was overcome by a feeling that he was being watched, as if every tick of every clock was the sound of blinking eyes. His prized Ticking Turtle edged towards him. The clock fitted into its shell chimed seven times. Rudolf stumbled backwards into the third chamber, *Artificialia,* where he housed his manmade treasures – ostrich-egg goblets, cups carved from rhinoceros horn, a life-size crystal lion, glass casts of lizards, a mechanical bronze spider, a figurine of a saint with a beating ruby heart. Here things seemed to be as they should, but he didn't dare venture inside the innermost chamber of automata. Instead, he stayed here, standing stock-still, hand resting on the shell of his ticking turtle.

Zuzana had never been close to Don Julius – he'd always been a bully and was often away at schools in other lands – but she felt wounded by news of his crime and death. She was still in shock. It didn't seem real: her own brother, her own flesh and blood, was a murderer.

She went to the window and in the distance saw the sky darken over the dense green of Stromovka Park. She didn't understand what had made Don Julius into such a monster, unless it was true what they said, that her whole family really was blighted by the madness her great grandmother had succumbed to. She wished Jan was here. She needed someone to talk to, but felt lonelier than ever. Her other brothers had been sent to stay with relatives in Spain, her mother had gone to Italy and her father seemed well beyond the reach of anyone's help. Beyond that of his closest aides, even Croll. She hadn't had the chance to tell him about Jan's serum, not with all the turmoil after Don Julius's death, but she couldn't wait any longer.

Zuzana hastened towards the alchemists' wing but as she approached Croll's offices, she hesitated. The entrance to her father's Cabinet of Curiosities was unattended. She looked around to be sure no one was there – it was odd; there was usually someone on guard – then she crept across the corridor to the great oak doors, and opened them.

Zuzana felt as if she'd entered a kingdom of giants. The scale of the first chamber was overwhelming. She'd never seen such a high ceiling, and certainly never one decorated with monkey skeletons. She didn't know what to explore first. Then she spied the mandrake in its bottle, and remembered how Jan had talked of the one he and his uncle had uprooted.

"Who's there?" bellowed Rudolf.

"It's Zuzana," she called, her voice wavering. She wasn't supposed to see her father unannounced, least of all here.

"Who?"

"Zuzana. Your daughter. I ... I won't disturb you."

"Come here."

Zuzana followed his voice through the second and into the third chamber and found him sitting on the floor in the dark with his ticking turtle.

"Ah, Zuzana," he smiled. "Zuzana. Sit with me, won't you?"

She breathed a sigh of relief; he wasn't angry.

Rudolf reached out and stroked her hair. "Isn't it shameful that until now I hadn't realised what a beautiful girl you are? I hardly ever see you, do I? I'm a terrible father. I blame myself for your brother's death. It's the bad blood of our line; be thankful you have more in common with your mother's side. Dear daughter, your father is losing his mind."

Zuzana wanted to embrace him, to make him better, but instead she just settled down beside him.

"Here, how do you like this?" he asked. "It was specially commissioned by your Italian grandfather for these chambers. Beneath all this gold is a real turtle. Dead, of course, but if you wind it up, it comes back to life. See!"

Zuzana felt as though she were the parent and he the child as her father pointed out and described favourite items from his collection. She was attentive and patient, and found the objects fascinating but, at the same time, thought there was something very sad about the way he sought comfort from them, as others found solace with friends.

"Father," she said softly, "why don't we light more candles? Or go for a walk in the courtyards? There's so much more to be enjoyed beyond these walls. What about people?" she asked. "Don't you think company is more precious than all these objects?"

Rudolf raised his head and looked at her. Zuzana knew she had to seize this moment.

"I heard you've been thinking about helping plague victims, Father. What would you say if I told you there might be a way to do that? To lessen their pain, to prolong their lives? You see, I've met someone. Someone special who's developed a serum. I've seen it halt the progress of the plague in a little girl who lives in the Ghetto. He's only about my age, an orphan, but was taught by his Viennese uncle. He's the kindest and noblest person I've ever met."

She paused to catch her breath.

"I think you'd like him. It would be hard for anyone not to."

Before Rudolf had a chance to respond, Croll appeared beside them.

"I wasn't expecting to see you here, your ladyship," he said. "I trust all's well? It seems you've been busy."

Zuzana jumped to her feet. "I was on my way to tell you."

"It's time for your medicine, sire," he continued. "You should be resting." He turned to Zuzana. "You shouldn't be upsetting your father with such wild declarations."

"But it's true," she protested. "I swear."

"I'll come to you as soon as I've tended to His Highness."

A short time later, Zuzana heard Croll's approach. She rushed to the door and ushered him inside.

"Don't worry. There's no one around," he assured her. "Now begin at the beginning. I want to know everything about the serum you spoke of."

Zuzana sat on the end of her bed and explained how she'd met Jan and taken him to the Place of the Black Bear; how he'd developed an elixir first concocted by his dead uncle; how he'd fled to Kutna Hora in search of his missing aunt, and how she'd seen an improvement in Miriam after she'd drunk the elixir.

"How do you know you can trust him?" asked Croll. "How can you be sure it's not a trick to coerce you into giving him food and money and a place to stay? I hope you've not been naive, your ladyship. Taken for a fool."

Zuzana sprang to her feet. "How dare you suggest that?" she cried. "I thought you'd listen. You said you understood why I go to the Ghetto."

"Forgive my directness, but you must understand that this puts me in a very difficult situation. The Emperor's daughter making unchaperoned visits to the Ghetto and housing strangers is irregular. Scandalous even, some might say."

Zuzana brushed her hair from her face. She wouldn't give up. "Come with me to see the girl," she pleaded.

"Very well," said Croll, for he knew that if what she'd said was true, incredible medical advances might be in the making. "Meet me by the Belvedere Gate in ten minutes."

They went to the Ghetto under cloak of darkness, Zuzana praying that Miriam was still showing signs of improvement, Croll imagining what the boy might have used to concoct this elixir.

Outside the tumbledown cottage Zuzana handed Croll a mask and knocked on the door.

"Who is it?" called Miriam's grandmother. Visitors were unheard of at this hour.

"It's me, Zuzana."

"Ah, our angel! Come in, come in. Is your friend, the young man, with you? We want to thank him, with all our heart and soul. Miriam has been much more comfortable since taking his medicine."

They ducked beneath the low doorway and saw Jacob shivering next to the meagre fire. He looked worse than ever. Zuzana wished he'd had some of the serum too.

"I've come with another friend, another doctor," she explained.

"I'd like to examine the child, if you'll permit," said Croll. "I'll try not to disturb her." He knelt at Miriam's side and inspected her neck. "Two or three weeks into the infection, I'd say."

"Actually, it started just over two months ago," said Jacob. "A few weeks before we buried her parents."

"I see," said Croll. "Interesting. And Zuzana, how do the swellings compare with when you last saw them?"

"They seem about the same to me," she replied. "Certainly no worse. Perhaps less bruised looking."

"There are no new swellings," Jacob added. "And her fever has gone down. Without your friend's medicine I think we would have lost her by now. She seemed close to the end."

"I need to meet this boy," said Croll.

Zuzana felt a rush of relief. But it was only fleeting, for she had no idea when Jan might return to Prague, or even if he was safe.

Chapter Eighteen
Within the Walls

After pleading with passers-by, then scouring the main market square of Kutna Hora, Jan eventually persuaded a woodsman bound for Prague to give him a lift. His thoughts turned to Zuzana as he scrambled aboard the open cart, pulling his coat over his head to protect himself from the rain. He hoped she wasn't still upset he'd left so suddenly, but he'd only been gone a day. They could visit Miriam together and decide what to do next, about the serum and finding Greta. As they gathered speed, Jan tried to make himself comfortable, which wasn't easy for the cart was laden with logs and sticks.

Their journey took them through Sedlec and Jan was reminded of the terrible sights he'd seen during this trip: the remains of the dead in the Chapel of Bones. The visions of murder and madness. The hanging body. The gloved hand slitting the still-warm flesh. The gushing blood. He felt he might be going mad himself.

As evening drew on the rain stopped and night came

calmly, and Jan was soothed by familiar sights. First the spire of St Vitus's Cathedral, then the Church of Our Lady Before Tyn as they pulled onto Old Town Square.

"You're home," called the woodsman.

"Thank you," Jan replied. He climbed from the cart, thanked the woodsman with a coin and headed to the Place of the Black Bear.

"Jan?" came a voice from across Tyn Courtyard.

Key in hand, poised to unlock the door, Jan froze. He didn't recognise the voice and was worried this might be a member of Zuzana's family, come to remove him from the house. The last thing he needed now was more trouble.

The voice called again, this time much closer. Jan felt a hand on his shoulder. He turned and saw a man dressed in the uniform of the castle guards.

"I've come at the request of Oswald Croll, of the Royal Court. You're to return to the castle with me."

"Why?" asked Jan. "There must be some mistake. What would he want with *me*?"

"Come, he is waiting."

Before he knew what was happening, Jan found himself seated in a royal carriage, on his way to the Imperial Court.

The castle really was like a city within a city, as Greta had said when they'd first arrived in Prague, although the scale was far bigger than Jan had imagined. They walked on and though it was late, it was still lively. All along Golden Lane the castle blacksmiths, armoury workers and farmers were at work, their pigs, goats and chickens pecking and snuffling around the straw-strewn inns.

Then they entered the main body of the castle, and Jan wondered how anyone found their way through the maze of corridors and passageways, the innumerable staircases and halls, suites and meeting rooms, libraries and galleries. He was shown into a room filled with globes and maps.

"Wait here," said the guard.

Moments later the door opened and Croll entered. Jan recognised him from the House of the Hidden.

"Be seated."

Petrified, Jan perched on the edge of an armchair.

Croll sat at a desk across the room. "Do you know who I am?"

"You're the Emperor's physician," Jan replied, his voice scarcely a whisper.

"That's right. And, as such, I'm keen to hear about your serum. Her ladyship, Zuzana, told me about it."

"Her *ladyship*? What do you mean? How do you know Zuzana?" asked Jan, momentarily forgetting his nervousness. If she knew Croll, why hadn't she mentioned it earlier? And why was Croll referring to her as "her ladyship"?

Croll stood, paused to scratch his mole. "I've known her a long time. She's the Emperor's daughter."

"What?!" Jan exclaimed, leaping to his feet. "The Emperor's daughter?"

"She has told me about her visits to the Ghetto, how she met you, how you've been developing an elixir of life."

Jan felt giddy as everything fell into place. The secrecy, the irregular visits. He sank back onto the chair. "She could have told me. She could have trusted me."

"Life in the royal court isn't easy. It's a life of rules and restrictions. Certain behaviour is frowned upon. Much is frowned upon," Croll corrected himself. "If she'd been caught leaving the castle grounds I don't doubt she'd have been sent away to family in Spain or Italy. You must understand why she had to conceal her identity."

Jan did understand, although he still wished she had told him. "Then Don Julius was her brother!" he realised. "May I see her, sir?" Though still reeling from this revelation, his main concern was for Zuzana's wellbeing. How must she be feeling, to have lost her brother, and learned he was a murderer?

"Is she all right?"

"She's well, considering, although she's been worried about you. But you're safe now, and she'll be glad to hear it. Now, the serum?" Croll asked. "That is, after all, why I brought you here."

Jan took a sample from his sack and handed it over. He held his breath as Croll opened the bottle, swirled it beneath his nose.

"Interesting aroma and consistency. I look forward to learning how you produce it. I've spent years trying to perfect my own formula to ward off the plague – a blend of toads and blood – but, from what Zuzana said, and what I saw in the Ghetto this evening, it seems you've progressed far further than I."

"I'm not sure about that, sir," said Jan. "But it has revived a number of insects and a dead bird."

"You're too modest. That would be excellent it itself, but it seems your potion has done much more. It appears to have rescued a child from the jaws of death."

His confidence rising, Jan sat upright. "Do you mean Miriam? Is she still alive?"

"She is. Most definitely."

"I … I don't know what to say. That's incredible. Zuzana was right. She believed in me. She suggested we give Miriam the elixir. Where I had doubt and fear, she had faith."

"She's a wise young woman and I trust her judgement, which along with witnessing the improvement in the girl's health, is why I'd like to invite you to work with me. The Emperor has charged me with implementing a programme to combat the plague, and I'd like you to be part of it."

"This is what I've dreamed of … but my aunt. I haven't seen her for weeks. I should keep searching. I went to Kutna Hora after her …"

"Her ladyship told me," Croll cut in. "I'm afraid I was partly responsible for Muller's appointment with Duke Frederick. Wherever your aunt might be, I'm sure she's far safer now than when she was with him. The guards will find her. You have my assurance."

"Thank you. *Thank* you. May I see Zuzana?"

"Not now," said Croll. "It's late. I'll try to arrange a meeting tomorrow, perhaps after I've introduced you to the other alchemists. I appreciate this is a lot to take in, so I'll have you shown to your chambers. Rest well. You'll need your wits about you in the morning."

A guard accompanied Jan to the rooms Croll had assigned him. They were directly beneath Mihulka Tower, where the Emperor's alchemists worked. Croll's words rang through his mind, over and over. *The Emperor has charged me with implementing a programme to combat the plague, and I'd like you to be part of it.*

Excited, but also anxious about having to fulfil such great expectations, Jan went to the narrow window slit. He could see the red roof of the Belvedere Palace opposite and Rudolf's gardens and Ball Game House. For the first time in months, he felt safe; it seemed the eyes of the unseen ogre were no longer upon him.

He looked around his new rooms. He had his own study, lined with bookshelves, and a large desk equipped with paper and ink. His sleeping area was furnished with an elegant dressing table and a bed bigger than any he'd seen. Jan lay down his head, hoping he'd see Zuzana soon. From what Croll had said he knew that living within the castle wouldn't necessarily make it easier, but he felt comforted to think she might be asleep only a few rooms away, maybe even thinking of him.

Chapter Nineteen
In the Tower of Transformation

Early next morning, Croll collected Jan from his room and took him up the winding staircase to Mihulka Tower.

"Don't let them intimidate you," he warned. "They're an arrogant bunch, as you might expect from the world's sharpest minds. You'll be by far the youngest, but you've no reason to be daunted."

Open-mouthed, Jan surveyed his new workplace. While Gustav's laboratory had been well-equipped, this seemed a thousand times more advanced. He wondered what remarkable discoveries his uncle might have made had he had access to everything here. He was struck by the smell of the unfamiliar gases and metals that burned constantly, by the complexity of the apparatus, by the earnest expressions on the alchemists' faces. He hoped they'd accept him.

Croll banged a table to attract their attention.

"I'd like to introduce you to a new member of the Royal Guild of Alchemists. This is Jan. Make him welcome. Here," he said, handing a purple-cloaked man a bottle of Jan's serum. "I want you to analyse this. It's already halted the progress of the plague in one person."

Jan watched the man take the bottle, pour out a sample and set about distilling it. While this was what he'd wanted – for his work to reach the world's most reputable people of science, to do the greatest possible good – it felt odd to think the serum was no longer just part of his private world. It had become public.

"I'll leave you to become familiar with your colleagues and their work," said Croll. "Bruno," he called to one of the men. "Jan will work alongside you today, while his elixir is assessed."

"As you wish," said Bruno, eyeing Jan. "But be warned, my work is not for novices. I seek to create new life from dead matter."

"I know a little about using mandrake roots to make living beings," said Jan anxiously, his eyelid twitching. "My uncle and I began an experiment. We were going to dry it in an oven, with verbena, to complete the process."

"Verbena? I've never heard of that technique."

"Then try it," ordered Croll. "Listen to him."

At noon, when the men stopped to eat the feast that had been brought from the castle kitchens, Croll returned to the tower and took Jan aside.

"Follow me."

"But what about Bruno? He's given me a task."

"You can return to that later. Someone would like to see you."

Jan couldn't help but smile as he followed Croll through the corridors. He'd scarcely stopped thinking about Zuzana since he'd left Prague, when they'd parted suddenly and awkwardly. So much had changed since then. He couldn't wait to see her.

As they walked, Croll helped Jan familiarise himself with his new home.

"Those stairs lead to the main library, and those to the Mannerist Art Gallery. The Great Hall is just through there. It's reserved for special events, like the feast the Emperor is hosting this evening. It's being held to welcome all newcomers to the castle, so your attendance is required. If an opportunity presents itself, I shall introduce you to the Emperor. And those doors lead to the Emperor's Cabinet of Curiosities, his private chambers. They take up the entire wing," he said, ushering Jan through a door.

While Jan waited, he noticed the room was lined with works of art: portraits of the Hapsburg family through the decades. There was a painting of Emperor Rudolf with his children around him. It was strange seeing Zuzana in formal pose, adorned in jewellery bearing royal insignia.

The door opened. He heard a shrill chirrup.

"Hello, Jan."

It was Greta and her peahen.

It would be wrong to say Jan was disappointed, but this wasn't at all who he'd expected. In an instant he felt once more the scrutiny of her stony stare. He caught his breath, steadied himself, realised what a relief it was to know she was well, and also here, in the castle!

"You're safe! I've been looking for you everywhere. What happened to you in the House of the Hidden? I've been so worried."

"I told you we'd find her," said Croll, smiling. "I shall leave you to become reacquainted.

Without thinking, Jan embraced Greta, forgetting their

usual formality.

"I can't believe you're here, that we're both here, in the *castle*. If only Gustav were alive. I started work in the alchemists' tower this morning. He'd have loved it."

"If he were alive I doubt either of us would be here," Greta replied. "We'd still be in Vienna. Tell me," she said, "is it true you know the Emperor's daughter? And have you met him?"

"Yes, I know Zuzana. But I haven't met the Emperor."

"Ah, but I have," Greta said, going to the door. She glanced back at Jan. "I hear the Emperor's hosting a banquet tonight and then, for the first time, I shall be served flesh skinned by another hand."

———— • ————

Greta went to the gardens she'd admired when she and Ignaz had performed their vanishing of the bullet. And as she walked, taking in the freshness of the afternoon – sun high, sky cloudless, flowers beginning to blossom – she was filled with a sense of belonging. From the corner of her eye she glimpsed Rudolf, outside the menagerie, keeping watch over his beloved lion. While it had once prowled its enclosure with majesty, it was now stretched on the ground, breathing irregularly, head resting on its paws.

Greta slipped towards the Emperor and heard him bemoan the beast's sickness. She was shocked at how much weaker he seemed since she'd last seen him. His back was bent and his hands trembled like an old man's.

But no wonder, Greta thought. She'd heard about Don Julius, that the brute's mother had fled to Italy. And she'd heard rumours of Rudolf's deterioration. But he was still the Emperor, and here was the opportunity she'd been waiting for.

"Forgive me for intruding," said Greta. "I can understand why its infirmity upsets you. I wish it a speedy recovery."

Rudolf turned with a start. "Where did you come from?" he said, frowning. Then he paused, distracted by the porcelain perfection of her complexion, captivated by the redness of her lips: rubies set in pearl.

"I think I know you," he said. "*Do* I?"

"We have met, and I'd hoped we'd meet again. Do you know what's afflicting him?" she asked. "Can anything be done?"

Rudolf's head dropped. "Both our ends are nigh. It was written in the stars."

"How can you be so sure?" asked Greta. "For me, these past few months have proved it's possible to transform one's destiny."

"Is that so?" asked Rudolf. Then, "When exactly did we meet?"

"I came with a man who made a silver bullet disappear."

"I remember!" His face softened. Greta's beauty and concern for his lion had endeared her to him. She had such poise, such striking features, and those eyes; he'd never seen so intense a gaze. "What brings you back? How did things fare with ... with Duke Frederick, wasn't it?"

"Not so well, but that's in the past. I'm here now." She smiled. "Your physician Croll has taken on my nephew as an alchemist. It's an honour to be in your presence, and your abode. We share a passion for beautiful objects."

Rudolf thought briefly of Zuzana, and what she had said about the value of companionship. This encounter had lightened his spirits.

"I could show you my curiosity chambers later, after the feast," Rudolf offered. "You shall be my guest."

"I'd be delighted," Greta smiled, outwardly reserved but inwardly rejoicing that she'd succeeded in captivating the Ruler of the World.

Chapter Twenty
The Truths That Hatched

As Jan filed into the Great Hall for the Emperor's banquet with his new colleagues, he felt a tug on his sleeve.

"Zuzana!"

"We only have a few moments. Come with me." She led Jan to an alcove, where they could talk unseen.

"I'm so happy to see you!" she said, her cheeks flushing. "I heard about what happened in Kutna Hora, but your aunt is here now, isn't she? Is she all right?"

"I think so," said Jan. "I only saw her briefly this afternoon."

"And how are you? How do you like it here?"

"I couldn't be better." Jan grinned. "I'm a court alchemist, my serum is being analysed by the best men in their field, and I know where Greta is. But what about you? Why didn't you tell me who you really are? And your brother; I'm so sorry about your brother."

"Thank you," said Zuzana, lowering her eyes. "I wanted to

tell you the truth, really. I almost told you when we were sat near Libuse's Bath. Do you remember? But you know now, and that's what matters, isn't it? You forgive me?"

"Of course. I understand. Tell me about Miriam. Has her condition really improved?"

"The fever had passed and there were no new lumps. The signs are good."

A gong sounded and the guests began to shuffle to their seats.

"I must go."

"Until soon?" asked Jan.

"Until soon," Zuzana nodded, stroking his hand. "I'll try and come to you later."

Jan found his place among the court chemists, physicians, alchemists and astrologers. While his companions helped themselves to the plentiful food laid out on golden platters and laughed at the clowns and tumblers, he looked to the head table and tried to catch Zuzana's eye. There she was, sitting beside her father – her father, the *Emperor*! Jan still couldn't believe it.

He couldn't take his eyes off her. She looked more beautiful than ever. While most of the guests were dressed in elaborate costumes, and dripping with jewels, Zuzana looked stunning in her simple white gown, hair hanging loosely about her shoulders, the lightest touch of rouge on her cheeks, a single sapphire suspended from a silver chain around her neck.

Then another figure appeared at the Emperor's side.

"It can't be," Jan gasped. But it was; Greta.

Jan watched as Rudolf turned to her and laid his lips on her gloved hand. He saw her whisper something in his ear. He saw Zuzana's puzzled expression as they rose from the table and left the room together.

After the feast Jan went to his rooms to study for his second day in Mihulka Tower but, try as he might, he was finding it impossible to concentrate on his book. The words swam before his eyes, making no sense to him. But it wasn't because he didn't understand their meaning; it was because his mind was somewhere else. It had been a day of surprises. Who would have thought Greta would have been found so soon, and that she'd make such an impression on the Emperor? And he was overjoyed to see Zuzana again. His heart raced at the thought of spending more time with her. He hoped they could visit Miriam together tomorrow. He'd ask Croll for permission.

Suddenly, the door burst open.

"Zuzana! I thought I'd have to wait much longer to see you ..."

"Father's been taken ill," she panted.

"What's wrong?" he asked, dropping his book.

Zuzana flung her arms around Jan's neck and broke down in tears. "I ... I think he's really lost his mind," she wept.

Jan stroked her hair. "What's happened?"

"He's shut himself in his chambers and won't stop raving about being attacked by a flock of wild birds. He says they've been sent by the Fates and the Furies to end his days. Please, come quick!"

They raced down the corridor and almost collided with Greta as she came from her rooms, clutching a basket.

"What's all the commotion?" she asked. "Where are you going?"

"To the chambers," said Jan. "It's the Emperor. He's sick." He turned to Zuzana. "Fetch Croll. I won't be a moment."

As Zuzana ran off, a gust of wind fanned the flames of the torches lining the corridor. As the light grew, Jan's blood ran cold as he recognised the emerald cloak Greta was swathed in.

"I've seen that before. Was it ... was it you I saw there? At the gallows."

"Observant, aren't you?"

"Why? Why would you take Ignaz's blood?"

Her stony grey eyes met his. "Don't you remember anything of your lessons?" she asked. "That the blood of the hanged possesses a potent property needed to nourish homunculi? To nourish my beauties," she added.

"I remember," said Jan, edging away. "But I don't understand."

"I think it's time some truths were told. That's the least I can do before sending you to your ruin, Jan. I chose to leave you at the House of the Hidden. Why do you think everything was packed and ready go when you returned from the graveyard? I'd *planned* to leave you in Vienna, to take your serum to Prague and find favour with the Emperor. Obviously that idea was spoiled when you returned, so instead I took my chance to escape while you were listening to Loew."

The colour drained from Jan's face. He felt weak, as if the intensity of her stare was sapping his very blood.

"While I initially thought Ignaz might enable me to make good connections in a new city, I soon realised he was no alchemist, and that your serum was useless too." She paused. "Still, Ignaz turned out to have quite a talent for trickery, so I encouraged him to work on his bullet-vanishing scam to gain access to the Emperor. That went to plan but rather than inviting us to join the Royal Court, we were only offered a position with a minor duke. As you can imagine, I was *deeply* dissatisfied with this turn of events, but when frail old Michael Sendiv turned up with his golden chain and magical red powder, and fell under my spell, I saw a way to turn this to my advantage."

"What do you mean?" asked Jan. He felt as if he'd been punched.

She laughed.

"It was I who robbed Sendiv of his riches. See," she said, pulling the chemist's golden chain from her basket and hanging it around Jan's neck.

He raised his hand to it, shivered on contact with the cold metal.

"I planted Ignaz's ring in the old man's room, knowing he'd be hanged, I'd be hailed a heroine and I could take his blood."

"You're ... you're a monster," cried Jan. "You had a man *hanged*? Why?"

"Surely you know that all things are poison and nothing is without poison, people included." She smiled. "It was all for this, for these." She drew back the cloth covering her basket to reveal a row of large blue eggs, each dappled with identical turquoise and purple specks. "So much more powerful than your serum."

Placing the basket on the floor, she took a vial of blood from her pocket and decanted a drop into every egg. One by one, they cracked open and a creature emerged from each. They seemed to be a half-bird, half-woman hybrid. Their heads were nuts with a single eye in the centre, like the tips of peahen feathers, and beautified with hair as silken and black as Greta's. Their torsos were human, but covered in green and blue plumage. Their arms were wings and their legs and feet were spindly like birds', but covered in soft white human skin.

"Perfection!" she exclaimed, placing one of the newly hatched creatures on the palm of her hand.

"What ... what *are* these? Where did they come from?"

"While you and Gustav were working on your elixir, I

hatched my own homunculi. Created in my own image, born of my own blood, they shall obey my every word."

Fig 13: Creature

"Wait ..." Somehow, despite her revelations, Jan knew she had made a terrible error. "You shouldn't be feeding them *blood*. You're mixing methods. The book said homunculi created from eggs will only obey and protect its creator in return for a diet of lavender seeds and earthworms. This is dangerous. Who knows what could happen? Have you ever fed them correctly?"

Ignoring his question, Greta paced back and forth. "This is exactly why I kept them a secret. I am sick of my life being mapped out by others. These are entirely under my control, as is mad Rudolf. I didn't even need to resort to using my mandrake love potion – yes, it was I who uprooted it, and I took the berries too! We shall be married and I shall have control of his kingdom, and be served by my bird-women," she said, gazing at the creatures that had gathered about her feet.

"As I speak, my first flock is nesting in his Cabinet of Curiosities, and those are already fully grown. It only takes them a few hours to reach their optimum size. I intend to make those my personal chambers and what an Empress wants, an Empress gets." So saying, she scooped her hybrids into the basket and began to scream down the corridor at the top of her voice. "Thief! Traitor!"

On their way to Rudolf, Croll and Zuzana heard Greta's screams and hastened to see what had happened.

"What's going on here?" Croll asked.

"He's a traitor!" Greta shrieked, looking at Jan. "He was involved in the attack on Michael Sendiv. See how he flaunts the great man's chain around his neck."

"That's not true!" shouted Jan. "She stole it from Michael Sendiv, not Ignaz. She had him hanged."

"Calm yourself," said Greta softly, "how can you accuse me, a meek-mannered woman, of such atrocities?"

Croll's blood ran cold. Had he been right to trust Jan? Had he been deceiving Zuzana all along?

"Look in her basket," said Jan, lunging towards Greta. A guard seized him. "It'll be Daliborka Tower for you, boy."

With that, Greta swept away.

Chapter Twenty-One
Battle of the Bird Ogress

"I want you to think very carefully before you do or say another word," Croll advised.

He removed the chain from Jan's neck.

"It wasn't me," Jan insisted. "I wasn't there when the robbery took place. I was still in Sedlec."

"I don't have time for this now."

"I *know* we don't have time," said Jan. "Greta's going to take over the castle with her creatures. I've seen the monstrous birds she's been creating. Let me stop her."

"You must listen to him," Zuzana insisted. "I heard Father raging about the birds."

"But we have reason to believe—"

"I don't care what *you* have reason to believe," Zuzana interrupted. "Someone has to rescue my father from the chamber. Let Jan try."

"Very well," Croll relented. "Release him. Zuzana, you're not to go inside. Do you hear me?"

Zuzana nodded and together they ran through the cold

corridors. The torches flickered wildly, as if a great storm were raging through the castle.

"I'll be waiting," said Zuzana. "Good luck."

As he stood there, outside the great oak doors, Jan suddenly felt completely overwhelmed. As if he was re-experiencing every intense moment he'd ever lived through. Each instance of love, loss, grief, anger and joy coursed through his veins. He'd never felt more alive, or more afraid. There he was, at the threshold to the heart of the Cabinet of Curiosities, the Emperor's innermost hall of *Naturalia, Scientifica and Artificialia*. He knew Greta would be here already, that he'd have to face both her and the creatures.

Jan stepped inside. The doors shut behind him. There was no going back.

It was dark inside, but he could make out the jagged outlines of Rudolf's collection of mechanical oddities, feats of both engineering and art. Machines that made haunting music that sounded like whistles of bone and tinkling china. Machines that sliced and chopped and jolted and span. Machines like hopping, jumping, darting animals. Machines that moved like humans. The whirr and click of their cogs and wheels was almost deafening, but not as deafening as the rising din of twittering birds. He felt something at his ankles. It was the peahen Gustav had created for Greta. Twitching and scratching, desperate to escape. It sickened Jan to think that Gustav's gift had been forced to play a part in her grotesque schemes.

Jan looked around. He could see neither Greta, nor the Emperor, nor the birds making that terrible noise. He rubbed his eyes. As they adjusted to the dark, he saw something move. It was Rudolf, cowering in a corner at the far end of the hall. His hands covered his head. His body swayed. His legs buckled beneath him.

"I'm coming, Your Highness," Jan called, still trying to work out where the bird noises were coming from.

Then, as he hastened towards Rudolf, he saw them. A flock of fully grown hybrids, a shimmering sea of feathers, closing in on the Emperor, each eye on the tip of each of their plumes intently fixed on him.

Suddenly, Greta appeared from among the creatures, still dressed in her cloak of jade but now also holding a jar of Milkweed Monarch butterflies. Jan realised in an instant that Ignaz wasn't the only man she'd sent to his death.

"It was you, wasn't it?" he gasped. "There was a butterfly in Gustav's room the morning we found him dead. You killed him by poisoning him with the butterfly."

"With Gustav my ambition was captive as a caged bird, but his death opened that cage. It released me. Jan, I killed Gustav, I killed Ignaz and I will kill you too."

"You're a beast," shouted Jan.

"That's no way to speak to a lady." Greta laughed, and began to chant.

"Your shells were earth, your white was water
Your membrane was air, your yolk was fire, and gold:
The heart of everything.
May you feed from his flesh as the plague fed on his parents!"

The birds scraped their claws on the floor, extended their wings and shrieked louder and louder.

"Go forth, Sweet Sisters of Vengeance! Soon your creator shall be crowned Queen of the City of Birds!"

But before she finished speaking, the bird-women swivelled round to face their maker.

"Go forth and destroy!" she screamed, stamping her feet. But their gaze remained on her.

Jan took this opportunity to go to the Emperor. Using all his might, he heaved him to his feet. Then he watched in horror as the hybrids strutted towards Greta, a mass of shimmering eyes and pointed beaks. He heard Gustav's warning: homunculi can turn on their creators if not given the utmost respect.

Greta was frozen to the spot. Her mouth opened but no sound came out. The creatures thrust forward, forcing her into the mechanical chair. A metal cage clanked down over her head and chest. She was trapped.

"Jan! Jan! Help me!" she screamed.

The bird-women surged forward and within moments she was buried beneath a flurry of feathers.

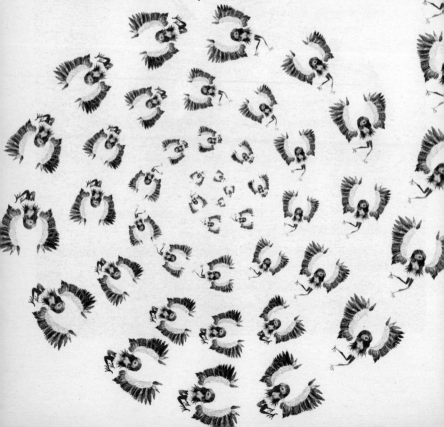

Epilogue
The World of the Heart

After the battle came a strange calmness, like the cool, fresh air that follows a storm. But while Jan felt as if the ogre had finally been slain and buried, his work was not over. In fact, it had only just begun.

Greta may have been killed by her own creations, but they were still in Rudolf's chambers, wreaking havoc, becoming ever stronger. It was only a matter of time before they scratched their way out. Or turn on us, Jan thought.

So, as Rabbi Loew had destroyed his golem by reversing the creation process, Jan knew he must do the same with Greta's creatures. But first he had to bring the Emperor to safety. He held Rudolf's arm and together they took their first steps towards the door. One by one, the birds abandoned their position at Greta's feet and clustered around them. Jan knew he had to act fast. He darted to the iron chair and wound up the mechanical twins. To begin with, the birds were transfixed by the automatons. But then, as their legs jerked up and their arms sprang out, fear set in and the birds took flight. The passage was clear, for the time being at least.

"You've done it!" Zuzana cried as Jan ushered Rudolf outside.

"Not quite," he said. "Fetch me lavender seeds and earthworms. And hurry. I don't know how long I can contain them for."

Jan stood still as a statue as he waited, watching the flock manically circling the Chamber. Once Zuzana had passed him the lavender and worms through an opening in the door, he stamped his feet to attract the creatures' attention. They swooped down and surrounded him. The reversal could commence.

They were calmed by the seeds and worms Jan gave them. They ceased their shrieking. And all the fury and spite and bitterness that had been fed to them by Greta was gone. Jan re-sealed each bird in an egg and, one by one, took them outside and buried them in dung in the castle grounds.

Next day, Jan went to the menagerie and fed Rudolf's lion a few drops of his elixir to bring the animal back to health, and he gave Gustav's peahen to the royal aviary.

"What can we do to reward you, Jan?" asked Croll. "The Emperor has said you can have anything you like. You saved him, saved our city and so shall your serum save many more people. What would you like? A title? Your own castle?"

Jan didn't need to think for long. "Thank you, but I don't need any of those things. This isn't the only city affected by the plague. I know you will make sure Prague is purged, but I must spread the power of the serum as far as I can. I must leave."

"Then I'm coming with you," said Zuzana.

They linked arms and stepped onto Castle Square and looked out over the city of Prague one last time.

It was a place whose towers and spires touched the stars, whose cellars and dungeons dug deep into the clay-rich soil.

It was a place of opposites and transformations.

A place where men could be made from mud, where the greatest wonders lay beyond the grimiest walls.

A place where ogres were defeated and friends were found.

And though this was the place that had given him his greatest friend, a place where his work would flourish, he knew in his heart it was right to move on.

Jan looked up and saw that the sky was filled with sparkling stars.

Notes on Inspiration

The beginnings

The initial spark of inspiration for *The Alchemist and the Angel* struck some years ago, while I was writing my first book. As I explored the history and stories woven into *Puppet Master,* I came across the eccentric Emperor Rudolf II, whose Cabinet of Curiosities, housed in Prague Castle was home to all manner of natural and manmade marvels; it captured my imagination.

Several visits to Prague later, once *Puppet Master* was published, I returned to researching Rudolf's fascinating world, and so *The Alchemist and the Angel* was born.

Magic and Marvels: the people, place and period of Renaissance Prague

Set in 1583, the book opens the moment Rudolf II, head of the Holy Roman Hapsburg Empire, declares he's returning the seat of Imperial power from Vienna to Prague. Already regarded as an axis of artistic and scientific innovation, this momentous act also made the city the political and cultural heart of the Empire.

Born in Vienna, but mostly raised in his Uncle Philip's court in Spain, Rudolf spoke several languages and possessed an insatiable thirst for art and arcane knowledge, which made Renaissance Prague his ideal home. At this time the city swarmed with world-leading practitioners of Natural Magick, astronomy and medicine, scholars seeking to decipher the secrets of the stars, create elixirs of eternal life and transform matter into gold.

While commonly regarded as an ineffectual ruler whose political errors led to the Thirty Years War and the eventual fragmentation of the Hapsburg Empire, Rudolf's contribution to history was his unparalleled patronage of the arts and science. His advisors included the Polish chemist Michael Sendivogius, German physician Michael Maier and Danish astrologer Tycho Brahe, eminent historical figures who appear in partly fictitious guise as patrons of the House of the Hidden in *The Alchmist and the Angel*. New artistic movements thrived here too, like Mannerism, as exemplified by the work of court portraitist, decorator and costume designer, Giuseppe Arcimboldo. Celebrated for his paintings of people formed from fruits, vegetables, flowers and fish, Arcimboldo's portrait of Rudolf as Vertumnus, Roman god of seasons and growth, replete with bulbous pear for a nose, rosy apples for cheeks and a beard of burrs, is arguably the most famous image of the Emperor.

Under Rudolf's direction Prague Castle was transformed into a living, breathing alchemical laboratory, a treasure trove of incomparably fine art and architecture, set in exquisitely landscaped grounds containing gardens, palaces, towers and a menagerie of animals from far-flung corners of the world. But that wasn't all. Beyond his patronage of alchemical and artistic endeavours lay an even deeper obsession: collecting.

Worlds of Wonder:
Cabinets of Curiosities and the impulse to collect

Reading about Rudolf's Cabinet of Curiosities – also known as *Wunderkammer* (Chambers/Cabinets of Wonder) and *Kunstkammer* (Chambers/Cabinets of Art) – was the catalyst that gave rise to The Alchemist and the Angel, and is embedded in the book's structure: as Jan's story develops, we journey deeper inside the Cabinet to the climax in the innermost chamber.

The word 'cabinet' originally referred to a room rather than a piece of furniture, and so Cabinets of Curiosities were a kind of early museum; a room or rooms in which the wealthy would display interesting objects from the fields of natural history, geology, archaeology, classical antiquity and art.

Rudolf's uncle, Archduke Ferdinand II, founded one of the most outstanding Renaissance Cabinets of Curiosity at Schloss Ambras in Austria. While many such collections have long since been plundered, their contents scattered around the world, Ferdinand's remains largely intact in its original location. It occupies a whole building in the palace and includes gold and silverware, unusual musical and scientific instruments, manuscripts, ethnographic curiosities, ivory and coral sculptures and vast armoury rooms. Ferdinand's particular interest was in anomalies of nature, and his most cherished exhibits included portraits of hair-covered cat-like people, a tree with antlers growing from it and a painting of a crippled dwarf dressed in the latest style. He also claimed to possess unicorn horns and the blood of Medusa. Its likely Ferdinand was partially responsible for inspiring his nephew's passion for collecting. Certainly some items from Schloss Ambras came into Rudolf's possession after his uncle's death and were displayed in Prague Castle, where the young ruler created the most incredible *Kunstkammer* of his day.

While Rudolf's Cabinet of Curiosities partly comprised pieces he'd inherited and partly gifts he'd been given by visiting diplomats and dignitaries, most of its meticulously classified and catalogued contents were acquired by specially appointed experts he'd send far and wide to search for new marvels. The collection was housed in a purpose-built gallery on the first floor of Prague Castle's Long Corridor that connected the Emperor's private quarters to Spanish Hall and New Hall. Sadly, it was neglected by Rudolf's successors and looted during the Thirty Years War, but to enter it in his day was to step into a world of breathtaking wonder. Each of the four principle chambers were packed with ornately decorated cabinets and cases containing everything from natural phenomena like gems and crystals, coral and shells, stuffed birds, mammals and fish (*naturalia*), to incredible scientific and astronomical apparatus (*scientifica*). The Emperor was as interested in the universe beyond as he was in the riches of Earth, and so amassed a matchless assortment of celestial globes, telescopes and timepieces.

The Cabinet was also home to a magnificent collection of man-made marvels (*artificialia*) like automatons and music machines, relics from antiquity and awe-inspiring oddities (*mirabilia, rara and curiosa*) including items purporting to be a six foot long unicorn horn, nails from Noah's Ark, the jawbone of a Siren, the feathers of a Phoenix and a bell inscribed with magical symbols Rudolf reportedly used to summon the dead. He also had a vast library and almost a thousand paintings.

While Cabinets of Curiosities were intended to be microcosms of the world, and to symbolise a ruler's all-powerful control of his realm, Rudolf's came to mean much more than that. It became his refuge from personal and political turmoil, a private universe he could control.

The Grime Beneath the Gold: poverty and plague in Rudolfine Prague

While Rudolf cultivated Prague's status as a vibrant centre of art and learning, all was not well in the court or the kingdom. The Emperor was tormented by irrational superstitions, hypochondria, deep melancholia and by the madness that had long afflicted his family line. His grandmother was known as Joanna the Mad, his mother and brother were said to have suffered from severe mental illness and his eldest son, Don Julius d'Austria, murdered a girl in the throes of one of his violent fits.

Sickness also lurked beyond the castle walls. While many talented alchemists thrived here, so too did an underworld populated by cut-throats and charlatans, ruthlessly ambitious people like Greta and Ignaz Muller, desperate for the fame and riches to be had from being hailed a successful scientist. Corruption and greed, disease and poverty lurked beneath the facade of splendour and opportunity. Ghetto-dwellers like Miriam's family lived especially hard lives, subject to laws that restricted their movements and trading power, and vulnerable to illnesses like the plague.

Men from Mandrakes, Men from Mud: legends and folktales, and the transformation of history

Like *Puppet Master*, *The Alchemist and the Angel* is partly concerned with things not being what they seem, and a blurring between the animate and inanimate, the living and the dead. From the golem myth of the man created from the mud of Prague's Vltava River, to the automatons in 'R.U.R', Karel Čapek's play set in a factory that produces artificial people, and the work of surrealist filmmaker Jan Švankmajer, the theme of objects coming to life and taking on human characteristics is widespread in Czech literature, art and the folktales woven into this book. And of course, transformation and change is the essence of alchemy.

Apart from Rudolf, *The Alchemist and the Angel* was inspired by several people and events from history. For example, the story of the hanging and Sendiv's attack is based on something that happened to the real Polish chemist Michael Sendivogius. The character of Ignaz Muller is derived from a German alchemist called Muhlenfels who stole Sendivogius' precious powder. Sedlec, the Village of Bones, is a real place too, and the methods Gustav, Jan and Greta use to create their homunculi are based on descriptions of ancient alchemical procedures. But history has been adapted here, re-spun to tell Jan's tale: the story of a boy caught up in a world of change and opportunity, trickery and wonder. A story inspired by a city and its legends.

Joanne Owen
London, December 2009